The Duke of Fire

Regency Hearts
Book 1

Jennifer Monroe

Chapter One

Though the sun shining through the large glass window cast its cozy warmth into the room, Miss Jane Harcourt felt anything but warm and cozy. It had been fourteen months since she had first arrived to accept the position as governess to Arthur Clarkson, and she found herself having grown quite fond of the boy.

"I'm going to miss you, Miss Jane," the boy said, his lower lip quivering and his eyes blinking back tears. "It will not be the same without you here."

Jane smiled at him. "And I will miss you," she replied. "I want you to promise me that you will continue working on your writing; that way, when you write your first book, I will be able to enjoy it."

This made Arthur produce a wide and proud grin, and Jane felt a surge of pride for the boy who had stolen her heart. In just over an hour's time, Jane would be leaving Poplar Estate to go to her cousin's house and search for a new place of employment. Although she wished more than anything to remain in her current position and continue lessons with the precocious child, she knew that to be impossible. Particular issues had arisen with the Earl of Waterwood as of late, which were only complicated that much more by the sharp looks Jane received from his wife, Lady Margaret Clarkson.

It was well known that the Earl indulged himself in gambling, spirits, and any woman who caught his eye, and the appreciative glances and silky words he had for Jane in the past months had forced Jane to offer her resignation a fortnight ago. Jane wished with all her heart she could remain with young Arthur, but she had heard too many tales of governesses falling prey to men such as Lord Clarkson, and she did not wish to be the object of such tales.

The door opened behind her, and the cold presence of the Earl greeted her before his voice echoed in the room.

"Arthur, leave us."

"Yes, Father," the boy responded in a quiet voice.

Jane turned and watched the boy leave, her heart breaking knowing it would be the last she would see of him.

The Earl stood as rigid as always, his head held high and a sneer on his lips that Jane assumed was permanently in place. The man was not a handsome man with his pointed features and overly-waxed hair, but he held himself with an arrogance that could not be denied. His eyes roamed over her, appraising her as if he were a choice cut of meat, causing Jane's stomach to churn.

"It continues to dismay me that you have chosen to leave me," he said in an oily voice that made Jane shiver in disgust. He took a step forward and stared down at her, his beady eyes boring into her. "I wonder, do you find yourself better than I?"

"No, My Lord," Jane replied. He was now standing directly before her, and although he meant to intimidate her, she refused to balk. The urge to recoil, however, was difficult to fight.

"Then, why are you leaving?"

"I feel my time here has come to an end," she explained, just as she had every day since giving notice. "I must move on to find work elsewhere."

The Earl moved forward again, forcing Jane to take a step back, bumping into a small cabinet, which hindered her retreat.

"I believe I know why you wish to leave," he whispered. "Yes, in all actuality, I do know the reason."

Jane lowered her head. The sight of him had become all that much more revolting over the past weeks since giving her notice as he increased his vile behavior toward her, his whispered comments in her ear became sickeningly sweet and on two occasions he had even pushed her into a dark corner and attempted to kiss her. Each time, Jane had refused his advances and hoped that her firm denials would make his stop.

However, he did not. Instead, his desirous pursuits increased, much like a cat hunting a mouse, and Jane caught him ogling, as if undressing her with his eyes. He made excuses to visit as she tutored Arthur, his hand resting on her shoulder in a familiar way or moving down her back.

She wished to put a stop to it, but the man was an Earl and she just a governess. If he were to have his way with her, which Jane had no doubt he would in due time, she could do nothing to stop him. His word would be taken over hers any day of the week.

"My Lord," Jane said in almost a whimper, "it has been a great honor to work in your home; however,…"

His fingers moved to her chin, and he lightly pulled her face up to look at him. "Jane, my dear," he whispered, preferring to call her by her Christian name without asking her permission first, "do not deny what you desire."

"Desire?" she asked. If desire felt like fear, then that was what she was feeling at this very moment. How she wished he would move away from her; she felt like a deer trapped by a wolf and at any moment that wolf would devour her.

"Yes," he replied, his voice still silky smooth, though it grated on her nerves. "It is what I desire, as well." He leaned in and pressed his lips to hers and her stomach threatened to bring up every meal she had eaten. If this was what it was like to kiss a man, she wanted nothing of it. His body pressed against hers, making breathing difficult, and she pushed against his chest, but the man was far too strong to be budged. At least the kiss had ended and she struggled to gasp in as much air as she could.

"Do not resist me," he said, his voice now husky. "I know what you need."

"Please!" she cried, though the words only came out in a whimper. "Let me go!"

He did not heed her; instead, his lips found hers once again, and the sickness returned sevenfold as his hand moved down her side to her hips.

"Henry!" a voice called from down the hall, making the man stop suddenly. "Henry, answer me at once!"

Lord Clarkson pushed away from Jane, whispering a threat of what had happened if she uttered a word, and relief washed over her.

She could hear Lady Clarkson mumbling to herself. "Where is that man?"

The Earl was moving toward the door, but before he was able to touch the doorknob, the door flew open and Lady Clarkson stood in the doorway. Her eyes fell on Jane and gave her one of the coldest looks Jane had ever seen, cold enough to have congealed her on the spot, if that were possible.

"Henry, you have a guest to see you in the study." Lady Clarkson never took her eyes off Jane as she spoke, and her husband did not seem to notice.

"Ah, Wadsworth is on time for once," Lord Clarkson said with a chuckle. He made no effort to turn to speak or acknowledge Jane before he walked past his wife and down the hall.

Lady Clarkson closed the door behind her husband and turned so quickly, Jane considered the woman may have damaged the rug beneath her feet. "I have asked that our carriage to be brought around and it will be here shortly," the woman said in a tight voice. "A kind gesture on my part, is it not?" The woman had been lovely at one time, Jane imagined, but she had not aged well. Lady Clarkson was only ten years Jane's elder, but she appeared much older than that. Her face was bedaubed with white face powder to such a point as to appear painted on, so much so that Jane was reminded of the attempts of a grandmother to keep her youthful looks as practiced in the last generation.

From the first day of arrival to Poplar Estate the Lady Clarkson had been nothing but dismissive of the new governess. However, she did not miss the lingering eye her husband had for Jane, and over time, the treatment the Countess had for Jane became sharper and crueler. Jane, however, found young Arthur a delight, despite the ill manners of his parents, and she abode their behavior so as to be allowed to stay on as governess to the boy.

It was true that the Countess offering a carriage to Jane was a kind gesture. In all honesty, the woman could have simply opened the door and forced Jane to walk to Bridgewater where her cousin Anne lived. Jane was certain the woman cared nothing for the fact it would have taken Jane two full days to make the trek. Perhaps Lady Clarkson did not hate her as much as she seemed.

"I am much appreciative of the kindness you and Lord Clarkson have shown me during my time here," Jane said.

Lady Clarkson stepped up in front of Jane and stopped only inches from her, her smile never reaching her eyes as she laid a hand on Jane's chest. "Why does your heart beat so?" she asked.

"Eagerness for the next part of my life, I presume," Jane lied, wondering if the Countess knew the Earl had just kissed her. Perhaps the guilt could be seen in Jane's eyes, for it certainly played in her soul despite the fact that she had done nothing to encourage the man's behavior.

"I do not presume many things, Jane," the Countess said in a low hiss. "I only deal in facts, and it is a fact that you have made advances toward my husband."

Jane shook her head adamantly, the accusation far from the truth. "That is not…"

Lady Clarkson forestalled her with a raise of her hand. "Do not forget your place or to whom you speak. Remember the education that was given you out of mercy." A look of amusement crossed the woman's face as she lifted a single brow. "Unless your mother was like you, one who pleased her employer in more ways than one." She nodded as if a realization had just come over her. "Yes, now I understand what she taught you, and she taught you well."

Anger and heartache rushed through Jane. Her mother had been a scullery maid, and the Marquess for whom she worked took pity on her, a young widow with a child. He had graciously allowed Jane to attend the same lessons his children received and not once, to Jane's recollection, had he ever asked for anything in return.

"My mother was a good woman," Jane said firmly, knowing that the words would only anger the Countess that much more but not caring if they did so.

"Perhaps she was," Lady Clarkson deigned, "but you are not. When you leave today, never mention of having been employed here."

Jane stared at the Countess aghast. "I cannot have your reference?" she asked, unable to believe the antagonism of this woman. "What will I do

5

when asked?"

"Oh, you may reference us, if you would like," Lady Clarkson replied in her regal tone. "However, if anyone asks, I will inform them how you have used your feminine wiles to tempt my husband and get him to take you to his bed. Or perhaps a tale of how you spent time with various male servants without regard for what such acts would do to my reputation, let alone your own." The maliciousness behind her smile matched the words she spoke and sent a shiver down Jane's spine. She had no doubt the woman spoke the truth. The Countess must have learned about her husband's advances, but as was common to those of the *ton*, the woman refused to place blame where it should have been placed—on the Earl himself.

Lady Clarkson moved aside. "Now, leave my house and wait outside for the carriage; I do not wish to lay eyes on you anymore." As Jane picked up her bag and made her way to the door, the Countess grabbed her arm. "And you had better pray our paths never cross again."

Jane gave the Countess a small curtsy, though the woman did not deserve such reverence, and walked out the door. She would miss Arthur so much it hurt, and she prayed the boy would remember the lessons of kindness she had taught him and never become like his parents. For the world did not need another self-absorbed, spoiled member of the *ton*.

***

The carriage moved along the road with a slight jostle as Jane looked out the window onto the fields of green passing by her. Her cousin Anne and her husband David would be welcoming her to their home within a few hours, a place meant for a short reprieve before she found new employment. However, without a reference, she feared that the time there would be much longer than she had originally planned. It was not that Anne, or her husband for that matter, would throw her out when they tired of her; they were not the type to turn away from helping a member of the family. Yet, Jane had never been one to impose herself on anyone, and her cousins did not have all that much money themselves.

Only a fool would attempt to reference the Earl after the threat Lady

Clarkson gave, and Jane was far from a fool. Anger filled her as her mind replayed the Earl accosting her with his kisses and his roaming hands. Did he believe he had the right to treat her thus simply because he was titled? Or was it because he was a man? Jane was not sure which was true, perhaps both when it came to Lord Clarkson, but this was not the first time she had been propositioned in such a way by a man.

Her employer before the Earl and Duchess of Waterwood had been a kind soul; however, his cousin, a man who would often visit, had made it known early on that he wanted her to visit his bed. Like Lord Clarkson, the man had commented on her beauty, saying that it was something that drove a man wild.

Jane found the idea completely preposterous. She was no beauty, not like the blond Venuses who wore their hair in tight curls and displayed deep-colored eyes of blue, green, or brown. No, her light gray eyes, in contrast, were almost transparent, a feature that had led to her to be ridiculed by other young girls, who spread rumors of her being in league with Lucifer himself. Her hair was the color of dark ash, a rather lackluster color in her opinion, and added to the jeers that were heaped upon her.

At the time, Jane did not understand what had been behind the cruel words of the other children. However, once she was grown, it occurred to her that perhaps it was more jealousy of her mental capabilities rather than how she looked that raised their ire. Regardless, they were correct in their assessment of her overall; she was a very plain woman. Every man who turned his head caused her to turn to see at whom he was smiling; it most certainly could not have been her.

Yet, her plainness did not matter in the end, for she had witnessed all too often during her time in the few households in which she had been employed, men only wanted one thing from a woman. Her innocence.

Men were like mad wolves frothing at the mouth, and once they had a woman in their teeth, such as Lord Clarkson had the Countess, they became bored and began to hunt for someone new. Jane had vowed never to partake in such a game, and as she approached spinsterhood, she welcomed it, for a life alone was far better than a life of watching someone you loved destroy you. The hassle alone of dismissing staff to keep them away from a husband would be enough in itself, but the heartache would be worse.

Jane had never known the love of a man. The only love she had ever encountered was that of her mother, who died six summers ago when Jane was sixteen. Though her mother's employer, the Marquess of Slipstone, had every right to throw Jane out, he had, in fact, done the opposite, allowing her to train with the governess to his young children. Remembering the kindness the man had shown her brought a smile to Jane's face. How she wished the Marquess were still alive and had not succumbed to illness this past year, for he would have taken her in without hesitation.

The carriage lurched, pulling Jane back to the present. She had not realized they had arrived in Bridgewater and the traffic had increased considerably. People strolled across the cobblestone streets, mindless of the many carriages that ambled along, and more than one driver spewed words at those who got in their way that made Jane's ears burn.

Not everyone had a destination, however. Upon hearing a child's cry, Jane shook her head as she looked out at a mother holding a child in her arms no older than five. Jane rang the bell to signal the driver to stop, and the man did so immediately, bringing another bout of curses from the driver behind them as that man made his way around the now halted carriage.

Jane stepped from the carriage before the driver had a chance to jump down to help her.

"Miss?" he said, clearly worried that she had asked him to stop. "Are ye all right?"

Jane gave him a quick smile. "I am fine. Just one moment, please." She beckoned to the woman, who approached timidly. Both she and the child beside her wore dresses made from what once had been burlap sacks and had so much dirt on their faces that, when the young girl turned, white streaks lined her cheeks where her tears had cleaned off the filth. Jane was uncertain what color the child's hair was, it was so matted and needed a thorough brushing. Her heart broke as she remembered being of the same age as the girl when her own father had died.

"Why are you crying, little one?" she asked quietly. The child said nothing but instead buried her face in her mother's skirts.

"I was working for the kind Mr. Harding," the woman replied instead, "but his estate is now in ruin, the money all but gone. We were forced to leave, as were the other servants."

"Mr. Harding? I am afraid I do not know him."

"I imagine you wouldn't, Miss," the woman said. "His estate is located in Reading."

"Reading? As in Berkshire?" That was over a hundred miles away.

"Yes, Miss. And we've been on the road ever since. We were lucky enough at times when a farmer allowed us to travel in the back of his buggy, but mostly we had to walk."

"You have been traveling for quite some time, I take it." The woman nodded and Jane saw the weariness in the woman's face underneath the dust and dirt of the road. "And where are you heading now?"

"My sister's place between here and Highbridge. Do you know it?"

Jane nodded. The road that led to the small village was just ahead and then another twenty miles beyond. They were so close now. She looked at the young woman and the babe beside her and made a quick decision. Turning and going to the driver of the carriage she called up to him. "Excuse me. I ask a favor to implore your mercy." The driver shook his head, but Jane would not allow the man to decline. "Please, it is not for me, but the woman and her young daughter."

The driver leaned over and looked from Jane to the woman and back again. "I ain't got no money," he said firmly.

"No, I ask for no money," Jane replied. "Take them to Highbridge. They have been on the road for quite some time now and are near starving. They are so close to their destination, I see no reason to force them to make these last miles on foot." The driver seemed hesitant. "Please. I will beg if need be."

"And what about you? The Countess'll grow suspicious if I'm late."

Jane looked down the road from where they stood. Anne's house was another ten miles in the opposite direction from Highbridge, but she could stand to walk ten miles, especially after how far this woman had traveled. "I will retrieve my things and walk the remainder of the way. This will free you to take this woman to Highbridge. We need not inform the Countess of the small detour and, in the end, you will have done a good deed."

The man signed and then nodded. Jane hurried back to the carriage, grabbed her single bag, and then turned to the woman. "Rest your feet," she said with a smile. "The driver will take you to Highbridge." She walked over and picked up the small bundle from the ground beside them and placed it under the seat of the carriage. Reaching into her pocket, she pulled out the few coins she carried. Her savings were pitiful, but someone else was in greater need than she, so she pressed them into the woman's hand. "May good fortune come your way."

The woman stared down at the coins and gasped. "Oh, thank you, Miss," she said, a tear running down her face. "I think it already has."

Jane helped the woman and signaled to the driver with a nod. He shook his head in wonderment before giving the reins a quick flick. The carriage moved forward and the young girl poked her head out the window to give Jane a shy wave and a wide smile. Jane waved back and let out a sigh as the carriage moved forward and was soon lost in the crowd.

As she began her trek, Jane wondered if good fortune would come to the woman and her daughter. They sorely needed it, and Jane hoped her part in helping them today was indeed the start of it. And hopefully, like them, her own luck would change, as well.

***

With bag in hand, Jane made her way down the dirt path that led to the small cottage belonging to her cousin Anne and her husband David. Washing hung from a cord strung between the house and a tall post, and a small garden sat just behind, several types of vegetables growing in straight lines in the well-weeded soil.

The door opened and Anne walked out, her blond hair tied back at the nape of her neck, several strands flying loose around her face. When she saw Jane, a smile crossed her face. "I thought I'd have heard the carriage," she said as she set the empty basket on the ground and looked past Jane. "Where is it?" She had always been one to get right to the point.

"It is a long story," Jane explained tiredly. "I have walked from Bridgewater, though, and my feet hurt, as does my back. Do you mind terribly if we go inside so I might put up my feet?"

Anne laughed. "The same Jane," she said, "always complaining." Although her words had bite, they were said with great affection, and she gave Jane a hug. "But you're still as lovely as ever." The woman was of the same age as Jane, that being two and twenty, and was most often found in good humor. However, that was where their similarities ended. Where Jane had darker hair, Anne's was light, almost blond, and her eyes were a distinct blue that would catch any man's eye. Anne was a true beauty, though Jane was not jealous of the woman. She had no cause to envy a person simply because of how they were created.

"You are too kind," Jane said.

"That I am, Love," Anne chuckled as she reached for Jane's bag. "Come inside and let's have you rest those feet."

The two-room cottage was small with a large room that included a living area, a counter that served as a kitchen, a large fireplace, two chairs with cushions in front of the fire and a small square table with two stools. A small pallet had been set up in the corner for Jane, and though not as comfortable as the tiny bed she had slept in during her time at Poplar Estate, it much better than sleeping directly on the floor. It would be more than adequate for her hopefully short stay.

"David has gone to Glasgow on business for Mr. Larkin," Anne explained as she hung a kettle on the hook over the fireplace. "He's inquiring about some wool or some such things I know nothing about."

"How wonderful," Jane replied as she took a seat on one of the stools at the table. "It seems Mr. Larkin has put some trust in your husband."

"That he has. He has made me proud, that man." The tone of her voice and the smile on her face expressed the love and admiration she had for her husband, and Jane was happy for her cousin. Perhaps a few men could make decent husbands after all.

Anne crinkled her brow. "You seem down," she said. "I thought you were ready to leave that…man."

Jane looked down at the floor and felt a flood of anger and humiliation rush through her. "I was, but this morning, he actually put his hands on me." Jane had written to Anne, telling her of the advances Lord Clarkson had been making, so the woman did not seem surprised when Jane explained what had transpired just before she left, including the boldness of the man to kiss her and the threat heaped upon her by the Countess. By the time she finished, exhaustion filled Jane, and it had nothing to do with her walk from Bridgewater.

"Thus, I will look for some sort of new position in the meantime," Jane explained. "I will not stay longer than is absolutely necessary; I would not wish to intrude on you and your husband."

Anne clicked her tongue. "You're welcome in my home for as long as you need," Anne assured her. "And don't worry about finding work immediately. You're far too smart to take any ole job, so you wait for the right one to come along." Her face softened and she placed a hand over Jane's. "Luck will come your way, Love; I can feel it."

"Do you think so?" Jane asked with no little skepticism.

Anne rose from her seat and grabbed her basket once again. "I'm sure of it," she said as she led Jane out the door. They headed to the line of clothes that swayed in the light breeze. "You'll just have to be ready to take it when it comes."

Jane laughed. "That will not be a problem," she said as she took the basket from Anne and held it as Anne removed the pegs from one of the dresses hanging on the line. "I'm ready for anything that comes my way."

Chapter Two

No sound could be heard in the long hallway, with the exception of his own footsteps, as Michael Blackstone, Fourth Duke of Hayfield, made his way to the dining room. No longer did he notice the fine tapestries that lined the walls of his Exeter estate, nor the delicate vases filled with fresh flowers that adorned the lacquered tables. None of the finery that surrounded him mattered anymore.

As he passed a large oak-framed mirror, he glanced at his reflection but a few seconds, long enough to see the waffling of scars which covered the right side of his face. They no longer surprised him, yet he continued to avoid looking at them if he did not have to. Not for the first time, the need to take down the mirror rushed through him, but just as the other wall hangings, Michael refused to remove it. Elizabeth had chosen that mirror to be placed in that specific place on the wall. Who was he to have it relocated to another place in the house? No, it would remain where it was, and he would simply have to do his best to either accept what fate had given him in the way of scars on his face, or avoid even the smallest glances at his reflection.

In all honesty, if the mirror had not already been in place when he and Samuel had taken up permanent residence in the house, it would have been removed first thing. However, Michael loathed the idea of making any changes in case Samuel took note, for it had been the boy's mother who had overseen the placing of the décor, and when it came to his son, he would do whatever it took to protect the boy from anything that would cause him heartache.

The subject of his thoughts was already seated, and although the boy had grown by leaps and bounds over the past few years, his body appeared small beside the massive table.

"Good morning, Samuel," Michael said as he took his seat at the head of the table.

"Good morning, Father," came Samuel's reply.

Michael did not miss the look of guilt that radiated from the boy's face. "What have you put in your pocket?" he asked, not unkindly. Michael remembered when he was a young boy of eight years and the sort of mischief into which he put himself.

The boy reluctantly pulled an apple tart, already flattened and falling to crumbs in his tiny hands, from his pocket. "I only wished to have something to snack on later," he said in a quiet voice.

Michael smiled at his son. "Have you ever been denied a tart?"

Samuel's eyes widened. "Yes, Father. Mrs. Curtis became angry when she caught me taking one from the kitchen just last month."

Michael had to hold back a chuckle. "Do you believe she punished you because you wished to eat a tart and not because you took it without asking first?"

Samuel sat considering this for several moments before a smile crossed his face. "I suppose so. I don't know for certain."

"Could it be she thought of it as stealing?"

This made Samuel gasp. "Stealing? I do not steal." His voice held an adamant tone, and Michael had to hold back a laugh.

"Of course you do not. You are a good boy who has respect for what is not his. However, if you have taken anything—even something that seems as insignificant as a tart—without permission, you are assuredly stealing. Now, I will have Mrs. Curtis save a tart for you for after your midday meal, that way you can have it as a treat. What do you say?"

The smile Samuel gave warmed Michael's heart. "Yes, I'd like that. Thank you, Father."

A footman set a plate of food in front of Michael, which contained the same fare the Duke ate every morning: a pickled herring and a roll with butter and preserves, today of which was strawberry. The footman returned only moments later with a pot of tea, which he poured for his Master.

"May I be excused?" Samuel asked politely. Though his hands were still, his feet swung under his chair, the need to be outside running building up inside him.

"Yes," Michael replied. "However, I expect you to keep out of trouble. Do you understand?"

"Yes, Father," Samuel replied happily before making his way toward the back of the house, more than likely off to entertain himself in the gardens in some form or another. The boy could spend hours exploring the grounds in search of insects or other treasures for which most boys his age craved.

Michael, unfortunately, had no time for adventure, for work awaited him in the study. Once he finished his morning meal, he took a seat at his desk, ready to pen a letter to a man concerning an import of silks from India. Once that was completed, he would take up his ledger. At one point, a bookkeeper had done such work; however, Michael preferred knowing where he stood financially without the need to call in another person to explain. It made him a better businessman, of that he was certain.

Sometime later, the sound of giggling caught his attention, and he walked to the window to peer into the gardens. The boy had grown at such a rate, he would be a man before Michael knew it. The thought of his one and only child one day leaving him brought a sadness to his heart, but knowing the great man his child would become, even before he inherited Michael's title, quickly dissolved the sorrow.

Michael glanced at his desk and decided that he had completed enough work for the time being. His son would be a child for only a short time, and if Michael did not take advantage of the time he had with the boy, he would live to regret it later in life.

The sun shone brightly on the grounds, its warmth pleasing as Michael made his way down the path. He found Samuel down on all fours rooting around with a stick in the soil of a flower bed, leaving behind broken stems and flower petals in his wake.

Michael sat on his haunches. "What are you in search of?" he asked, making the poor boy jump in startlement. He had attempted to keep his voice quiet, but Samuel was so engaged and so focused on his task, he had apparently not heard his father's approach. Furthermore, more than likely the boy thought it was Barnard rather than his father who had caught him in the act of destroying the flower bed.

When the boy turned, he smiled. "Creatures," he replied to the question Michael had asked, as if his father should know what his son was doing. "I have not found any yet, but I do hope I can." Then his face took on a serious look, as did the tone in his voice." I will not hurt them, Father," he promised. "I only wish to see what they are doing."

Michael smiled at his son, amazed at how much the boy resembled his mother. Granted, Samuel had inherited his father's dark, unruly hair, but his blue eyes looked so much like his mother's, Michael could almost imagine her living behind them. "Do not worry, my son. I know you would not hurt them in any way, but perhaps it would be best if you let them be so they can continue their work. What think you?"

Samuel pursed his lips in thought for a moment and then gave a quick nod. "Yes, that would be best." He filled in the hole he had made with the stick and did his best to replant the now broken plants into the ground. "There. I will come back tomorrow to see if any creatures come out to take in the sun. Do you think they take in the sun like us, Father?"

Michael laughed. "I suspect some do," he replied as he helped Samuel stand. "Come, let us get you cleaned up. You do not want to displease Mrs. Fredericks now, do you?"

Samuel shook his head and took Michael's hand. "Father?" he said as they made their way down the path toward the house. "Will I be getting a new governess?"

"Yes, eventually."

"When?" the boy asked and then quickly added, "Not that I believe I still need a governess, but..." he looked up at his father with sad eyes, "I miss Miss Hester already."

"Yes, I know you do," Michael replied. "But sometimes things happen in life that make people move on."

Samuel nodded wisely. "You know, if I could help Miss Hester, I would," he said firmly.

Michael smiled again. "I know you would. You have a kind heart."

"Like my mother?"

The innocent question tore at Michael's heart. "Yes, like your mother,"

16

he replied quietly.

The two continued their trek to the house, passing one of the gardeners, who was busy tending to a bed of roses. Michael spared no expense when it came to the gardens, for it had been a favorite place for his late wife.

"Would you tell me a story about her?" Samuel asked as they came to a stop near a bench that had been set under one of the larger trees beside a side gate. He did not need to ask to know Samuel meant his mother.

Michael smiled at the boy as he sat on the bench. His son's eagerness was evident by the wide grin he held. "Very well," Michael replied, patting the empty space beside him on the bench. He reached into a pocket and withdrew a handkerchief. "Do you see this?" he asked the boy, pointing to an embroidered leaf.

"Yes," Samuel replied.

"Your mother made this handkerchief," Michael explained. "Did you know that your mother was the best embroiderer in all of England?"

Samuel's eyes grew to the size of saucers. "She was?" he asked.

"Indeed. However, she knew her gift was not meant only for us but to be shared with everyone."

Samuel ran his finger across the stitching lovingly. "She wanted you to let everyone see it?" he asked.

Michael chuckled. "Not exactly. What she wanted to do was embroider enough of these to give to every orphan in England. That way, those without much could at least have something beautiful. Do you understand why she would do such a thing?"

The look Samuel gave could only be described as one of pride and awe. "Because she was a nice person?"

"Yes, that is part of it," Michael said. "However, your mother also believed, as do I, that there are those who need hope in life. Many people are not as fortunate as we, so giving them something, even a handkerchief, might make them happy." He placed the handkerchief into his son's hand. "Now, today, I give you this. Keep it close to you as a reminder of what good looks like."

Samuel gazed down at the piece of cloth as if Michael had offered him the most precious of gifts. "Thank you, Father," he said in a voice filled with awe. "I will keep it with me always."

17

Michael pulled Samuel in for a hug and then kissed his cheek.

Samuel said nothing for some time. Then he reached up and ran his hand along the scars that covered the right side of Michael's face. "Will I be getting a new governess soon?" Samuel asked once again as he allowed his hand to fall to his lap.

Michael sighed. "I hope so, Son." Yet, he feared the wait would be longer than either would like, for reasons Michael did not wish to explain.

***

Michael glanced out the window of his office watching as Samuel talked to one of the servants. It had been a fortnight gone since he had Jenkins send word out to the appropriate venues to find a new governess, and as he expected, not a single person had inquired after the job.

"The boy has learned enough so far in his young life and is much too old for a governess as it is," Robert, Michael's younger brother, said from the armchair before the empty fireplace. "You worry needlessly. He is a Blackstone; learning will come to him naturally."

Michael continued to peer out the window as he pondered his brother's words. "He is exceptionally bright," he said finally, "there is no doubt about that. However, he will need to continue his education. Unfortunately, I am beginning to believe I will need to search for someone who is not of this area." He turned to face his brother and sighed. Too much more important topics needed to be discussed for him to concern himself with finding his son a governess. That would happen despite his worry. "So, what is it you wished to see me about?" he asked.

Robert was three years younger than Michael and had the same dark hair and eyes, though his brother's hair was nowhere near the length Michael kept. Nor was it as unruly. Some would have considered the man quite handsome, much more so than Michael, even before he became disfigured, but Michael held no envy for the man. For whatever reason, God had granted Robert with a face free of any blemishes, and for that Michael was grateful. At least the man did not have to endure the stares and comments given behind hands and open fans that Michael had before he had closed himself into his estate.

"The carriage business in town," Robert said with a grin that broke across his face. "I have spoken again to the owner, and he is prepared to sell it to us."

Michael nodded as he took a seat behind the desk. "So, you have managed to convince the man to sell. But I wonder; at what cost?"

Robert laughed, a shake to his head. "Your fortune is vast and your coffers grow daily. Why do you worry so much about money?"

Michael tapped his fingers on the desk. It was not that he cared all that much for the money in general, not as much as his brother implied; however, the fees Robert required for conducting business had grown with every transaction. How could any man survive when money seemed to leak from every pore?

Robert must have sensed Michaels concerns, for he let out a long, heavy sigh. "Very well. If you wish to present yourself to the *ton* and let the rumors increase, then by all means, do so. I have spent two months of my life procuring this arrangement for you, and all I ask in return is a small fee for my time. If that is too much to ask…"

With a raise of his hand, Michael interrupted. "No, you make a good point. You cannot work for free, and your time is well worth the business you are able to acquire." He looked over his desktop in search of his banking book. Confusion came to him when he did not see it when it had been there just a short time ago. "My banking book?"

"You set it over there," Robert replied with a motion to the bookcase along the wall by the door.

Michael stood and walked over to the bookcase. The brown leather ledger lay on the self in front of a line of fine books that had once belonged to his father, some of his favorite titles amongst them. "How did this end up here?" he asked no one in particular. "I do not recall moving it from my desk before you came, and I was near the window when you arrived."

His brother took a step back, his jaw clenched. "If you wish to call me a liar, Brother, then do so outright. I do not understand why you have directed your rage at me when I simply informed you of what I saw."

Guilt filled Michael. It was not the fault of his brother that he was going mad. The misplaced ledger was just one of the latest in Michael's mismanagement. Business arrangements forgotten, money missing, items misplaced, so many issues had presented themselves with little explanation for why they were not as he had thought he had left them. Just last week it had been the mirror in his bedroom that had been moved from in front of the far wall to before the window that overlooked the garden. However, after questioning everyone in the household, none admitted to moving it. Yes, Michael was slowly going mad, and the thought of that happening and him leaving Samuel alone terrified him. The boy had already lost his mother; how would he be able to endure the loss of his father, as well?

"It was not my intention to name you a liar," Michael said as he headed back to his desk with the banking book in hand. "Forgive me. I fear at times my mind is not as sharp as it once was."

Robert came to stand in front of the desk, his voice now kind. "We will forget this ever happened," he said as he placed his hands flat on the desktop. "I know the stress and guilt that plagues you on a daily basis. It is too much with which a man should have to cope."

Michael opened the banking book. His brother was right; the guilt of not being able to save his wife tore at his heart daily. It had not only brought shame upon his soul, but now he stood shamed before the *ton*, as well. Although he was a Duke and no one would ever refuse a request he might make for them to come to his estate, Michael sent no invitation, nor did he accept any, and he never planned to. It was why he had not left his home in five years and why Robert was now not only his business partner, but also his spokesman.

After writing out a cheque, Michael handed the paper to Robert. "Will you stay and dine with Samuel and me this evening?" he asked as he closed the banking book and leaned back in his chair.

"I am afraid I cannot," came Robert's reply. "I must complete this deal as soon as possible so your new business is secure. Plus, tomorrow I am headed to Catherine's once again."

"You will marry her soon, I suppose?"

Robert grinned. "I will," he replied. "But..." he patted his jacket pocket where he had placed the cheque Michael had given him, "I must secure my brother and nephew's future first."

Michael smiled, thankful that Robert was looking out for him, as he always did. Without his brother, Michael considered he might have lost everything. "Journey well. I shall see you soon."

Robert shook Michael's hand, gave him a quick nod, and headed out the door.

Once Robert was gone, Michael stood back up and returned to the window. As he watched his son laughing as he played with a rock in his hand, sadness overtook him. How long would it be before the madness took over Michael completely? The thought of Samuel witnessing such travesty churned his stomach.

Shoving away the thought, he was determined that no matter how much time of sanity he had left, he would make the best of it while he had the chance, for nothing mattered more than the health and welfare of his only child and heir to the vast fortune Michael currently owned.

Chapter Three

Fastening the burlap dress to the line that hung between the house and post, Jane stood back and wiped a bead of sweat from her brow. She had been at the home of her cousin for three weeks now, and though Anne had on many occasions told her otherwise, Jane knew she had long overstayed her welcome. It was not so much anything in Anne's words or demeanor that convinced Jane of this, but those of the woman's husband David. Although the man smiled at Jane when he knew she was looking, he had made subtle hints about Jane finding work during various conversations that made Jane see he wished to have her on her way as soon as possible.

Jane could not blame the man for wishing to have his home returned to its previous quiet, for with Jane sleeping on the small pallet in the main living area, the couple was unable to participate in those things that married people did when they were alone. As a matter of fact, just the previous evening, Jane had bit her tongue when she heard Anne tell off David when he tried to kiss her in Jane's presence.

Letting out a sigh, Jane turned to see David and Anne approaching. She greeted them, but David ignored her as he went inside. Anne, however, returned Jane's greeting with a hug.

"I have some wonderful news, Love," Anne said as she slipped an arm through Jane's and led her to a small brook that trickled through a patch of land behind the house.

"Oh?" Jane asked. "Did you find a man for me to wed so you can rid yourself of me?" This brought on a bout of laughter from the two women; teasing one another was one of their greatest pleasures.

They stopped at the bank of the brook, and Jane watched the water amble over the rocks that lay in its bed.

"The cousin of a friend of mine knows a man, a Duke as it were, who is in need of a governess. The pay is nearly double of that which you made with your previous employer."

Jane smiled as her heart raced. Nearly double? That amount of money was unheard of. And the things she could do with that pay! She might even be able to save to purchase her own cottage one day.

"That is wonderful!" she exclaimed. Then an idea struck her and she felt a wariness overtake her. "Why would he offer such extravagant pay? Are his children so difficult that they have run off their previous governesses?"

Anne let out a deep sigh, which only heightened Jane's anxiety and made her that much more suspicious. "Before I tell you, I want you to know that I do not wish you to leave," her cousin said, a pleading to her voice.

"I know," Jane whispered. "I realize David wishes me to be gone, and I do not blame him. You both have been more than gracious to allow me to stay with you, and I do not wish to intrude any longer."

"Oh, David is fine," Anne said with a wave of her hand. "To be honest, it gives me a well-deserved break from his antics at night." This made them both giggle.

"Very well, then. Who is this Duke? Do I know him?"

"Well, I do not believe you have ever met him, nor seen him," Anne replied. Then she paused, and Jane waited with impatience. Would the woman ever get to the point? "It is the Duke of Hayfield."

Jane's heart raced and she shook her head slowly. "The Duke of Fire?" she whispered. "How could anyone work for such a beast?" It was true that she had never met or seen the man many referred to as the Duke of Fire, but he had heard of the man. Stories said that five years earlier, the wife of the Duke had been killed in a fire set by none other than the Duke himself. Word had spread that he had not been as quick as he should have been once the fire had been set, thus leaving his body covered in horrible burns. Why he had killed the Duchess of Hayfield was unknown to anyone outside of his intimate circle; however, the prevalent thought was that he was covering up an affair, and the servant girl with whom he had been having that affair had died in the fire alongside the man's wife.

23

"Jane," Anne said as she placed her hand over Jane's, "the money is good, but I fear you being around such a dangerous man. If you don't wish to go, know that you may remain here until something better comes along. If David complains about it, I'll knock some sense into him one way or another."

Jane nodded as she turned back to the brook. It could be dangerous, but what else could she do? If she continued to live here, it would only cause that much more discord between David and Anne, and Jane did not wish that to happen. Her meager savings was all but gone, and she could not burden her cousins for much longer. Plus, she had no references to give, so this might be the only chance of securing a job and relieving the burden she was placing on her cousin.

"No, I will go," Jane said finally. "I need the work, and you two need your home returned to you."

Anne hugged her tightly and kissed her cheek. "If you do work for him, guard yourself at all times. His brother visits often, from what I've heard, but I understand that the Duke might be going mad. If that is the case, even with his brother's help, he may become even more dangerous than he already is." She leaned in and lowered her voice. "I hear that he keeps his hair unnaturally long and unkempt and that he speaks to himself. It is why he no longer leaves Wellesley Manor and has not been seen since the fire."

Jane considered her cousin's words. "I will be careful, I promise. If I can, I will keep my distance from the man and my wits about me."

Anne hugged her again. "Good. See that you do."

"And if must escape in the night?"

Anne smiled. "Then you will return here."

Jane returned Anne's smile. "Very well. I will send word first thing tomorrow that I would like to interview for the position. Hopefully, he needs someone so desperately that he will overlook my lack of references."

"We can only hope," came Anne's reply.

The two women headed back to the cottage. Madman or not, Jane desperately needed the money that was being offered. She just hoped that if she did work for the Duke of Fire, she would not become as mad as he.

***

Although the road leading to the estate appeared as any other road with its line of trees flanking the hardened ground that had been covered in white stones, this one was far different—it led to the Duke of Fire.

Jane moved along, her footsteps not as hurried as they had been when she began the relatively short journey from the home of her cousin to Wellesley Manor, and she wondered if it had been a mistake coming here. Would the Duke torment her as he had his wife? Or would she wake one night with the house ablaze and the madman laughing as he sought to kill more people who he felt had wronged him in some way? However, despite the desperate thoughts that went through her mind, she continued her trek, for she had nowhere else to go.

All thoughts left her mind when her destination came into view. The word magnificent did no justice as she stared at the massive structure that made up Wellesley Manor. The windows on the front of the house showed at least three stories and two wings, one on either side that created a U-shape. A large marble fountain bubbled in the middle of a round grassy area, the driveway circling it completely. At each corner that connected the protruding wings to the main part of the house was a round turret with crenellations and merlons alternating at the top that made up the battlements and reminded Jane of teeth jutting from the top. Behind the battlements stood a single man who gazed down upon her with interest, but neither raised his weapon in defense. More than likely they did not see a single woman walking toward the house as any sort of threat, nor should they. Regardless, Jane shivered at the thought of one of them firing a warning shot at her with what she imagined was a crossbow or a rifle of some sort.

The facade of the building was painted white and trimmed in black. Rich green ivy covered much of the white, and the shrubbery along the front was neatly trimmed. Perhaps the madman inside enjoyed giving the appearance of sanity, or so Jane wondered as she resumed her steps when she realized she had halted to stare in amazement.

When she got to the door, she let out a deep breath in an attempt to calm her nerves. Her heart jumped as the door opened and a liveried man in his middle years with silver hair stood at attention in the doorway.

"Miss Jane Harcourt?" the man asked, his voice as stiff as his posture.

"Yes," she replied in nearly a whisper.

The man took a step back. "Come in. His Grace is expecting you."

Jane stepped past the man she realized was the butler into a large foyer. A massive staircase rose along the far wall surrounded by numerous paintings of battles, some Jane recognized from various studies in history. The gray marble floor shone and contrasted with the dark stained table that sat in the middle of the room, a large vase filled with flowers arranged just so on it.

"This way," the butler said with some annoyance.

Jane nodded and followed the man down a hallway. They stopped before an open door halfway down the hall and the butler tapped on the door jam.

"Come!" called out a voice from within.

Once again, Jane was taken with the room she entered, a library to be sure. Tall oak bookcases housing hundreds of tomes lined two of the walls, a mix of greens and browns as well as a few blacks.

"Your Grace," came the butler's nasally tone, "Miss Jane Harcourt."

"Thank you, Jenkins." The voice came from a man standing at a large window, long, dark hair hanging down his broad back not as unkempt as she had heard. Jenkins walked past her and then closed the door, leaving her alone with the man she presumed was the Duke of Fire.

Fear coursed through Jane and she considered turning and running away. However, before she could decide to do so, the voice from the window echoed in the room.

"Miss Harcourt, please take a seat."

Jane nodded and went to a single chair that sat facing the window. "Thank you, Your Grace," she said before sitting. She smoothed her skirts and sat up straight wondering if the man had any plans to turn and face her. Something inside held a curiosity of how he looked, for the stories had been terrifying, to say the least. However, she pushed those thoughts aside; she was not one to hold an interest in the oddities of the world. The reality was that she needed this position, and seeing her employer as a circus curiosity was repulsing to her.

"Do you thank me for the offer of the chair?" he asked.

Jane was taken aback. What a strange question. Aloud she said, "Yes, Your Grace. As well as the opportunity to interview with you." She could not stop her eyes from roaming over the bookcases as she wondered if he possessed titles in the sciences. She knew she would never be allowed to peruse them, but the curiosity remained nonetheless.

"Do you read much?" he asked.

Jane felt the heat rise in her cheeks. He had to have noticed her interest in the books when the reason for her being there was to interview. "Not as often as I would like," she replied with all honestly. "Although, when I have the time, I do love to read. Unfortunately, the cost of books is much higher than I can afford, but I do try to buy a book whenever I am able."

He turned his head to the side, but Jane could not see his face through the hair that hung in front of it.

"They are a sum indeed," he said. "However, we are not hear to discuss the cost of books but rather the education of my son Samuel."

Jane nodded and wondered if the kindness she heard in his voice was a ruse, a way to trap someone such as herself in his web, much like a siren would a man on the sea. She was reminded of her cousin's words and she raised her guard to protect herself just in case.

"Tell me about your former employer," he said, still hiding behind his hair. "It was the Earl of Waterwood, if I am not mistaken."

Jane stared at the desk as she swallowed hard, her heart beating against her chest. How did he already know what had transpired in the man's employ? "I…well, yes, Your Grace, he was my former employer." She could not raise her voice above a whisper. Perhaps it was her way of not allowing him to hear her so she did not have to answer his questions concerning the Earl.

Then the Duke moved the hair that hung in front of his face, though he remained turned away from her, and Jane gasped despite the fact that she had hoped she would not. What she saw was a stately face with smooth skin and a strong jawline. This man was handsome, and despite what others said, he did not appear to be a murderer. Not that Jane had many, if any, interactions with murderers to know the difference. Regardless, he did not seem as evil and savage as she had expected him to be.

"I pity anyone who would be forced to work for a man such as he," the Duke said. "Tell me your philosophy of teaching, if you will, Miss Harcourt. The education of my son is very important to me."

Jane sat up straight in her chair. "My philosophy is simple. Teach from a book as well as the heart, for both have wisdom in their own way, if applied correctly."

The Duke nodded once and then turned to once again face the window.

"Very well, then. You know of the pay I am willing to give if you should accept the position?"

"Indeed, Your Grace. It is a very generous wage."

"The cost of my son's education knows no bounds, Miss Harcourt," the man said. He paused and then continued. "Several people have already told me of your past. Is it true that a Marquess allowed you to learn from his own children's tutor?"

Again, Jane was surprised by what this man already knew about her. "Yes, it is true. I was very fortunate that he allowed me to learn; it has served me very well."

At first, the Duke did not respond. However, he finally let out a heavy sigh and said, "Would you like to remain here at Wellesley Manor and teach my son?"

Jane's mind raced. This was her last chance to leave, to run far away from a man said to be a killer. However, where would she go and what would she do? This was an opportunity to make money and save for her own cottage, and she would not let the rumor wheel keep her from reaching her dreams.

"Yes, I would like that," she replied with a firmness that did not match the turmoil in her stomach.

"Excellent. Let me introduce you to my son. We can talk about the specific details of your employment afterward."

Jane stood just as the Duke turned around to face her straight on. Expecting to finally see the damage that was said to cover his face, Jane was uncertain if she felt relief or disappointment that his hair fell over what she had hoped to see. He did not look up as he walked past her, and Jane followed the man as she wondered what his son was like.

***

"Father!" the young boy cried, and Jane felt her heart soar. He was the most handsome boy she had ever seen, with dark hair and adorable blue eyes. When he saw Jane, he straightened his back in a formal fashion that made him all that more endearing.

"Samuel," the Duke said as he and Jane walked up, "this is Miss Jane Harcourt. She will be your new governess."

The boy smiled and then bowed with such rigidity, Jane covered her mouth to halt the laugh that threatened to erupt. "It is very nice to meet you, Miss Harcourt. My name is Samuel."

"I am pleased to meet you, as well, Samuel," Jane said in reply. "Are you excited to begin your studies once again?"

The boy nodded, his smile widening. "I am. My maths are very good, although I would like to become a better reader."

"Well, we will make sure it improves, then," Jane said, which only increased the boy's grin.

"Samuel, please return to the house," the Duke said. "I wish to speak to Miss Harcourt alone."

Samuel walked away, and Jane could not help but smile after him. When the boy was out of sight, she turned back to the Duke. Although it was not appropriate for a woman to look at a man so, she could not turn her attention from how broad his chest seemed under his coat and the well-defined muscles under the sleeves. However, when he turned, she returned her gaze to the floor.

"My carriage can take you back to your home to retrieve your things," the Duke said. "If you would like, you may move into your rooms tonight. Everything you will need will be provided to you, of course. As to the education of my son, I have the materials necessary for you to use in his instruction. However, if you are in need of anything more, please do not hesitate to ask."

"Thank you, Your Grace," Jane replied without looking at the man. "I will return this night to settle into my new rooms. As to the education Samuel will receive, I look forward to such instruction."

The silence in the room stretched for so long, Jane wondered if she had said something wrong. Finally, the Duke spoke. "Why do you look at the ground when you speak?" he asked, not unkindly. "Are the rumors about me so terrible they make it impossible for you to look at me?"

Jane was taken aback by the question. It was true she did not look him directly in the face, but it had nothing to do with the rumors she had heard. She was not one to gossip on a regular basis, though listening to the occasional words spoken among those around her had helped her in various ways in the past. Despite that fact, it was a rarity indeed if she allowed what she heard to be repeated from her lips. Only those with a low opinion of themselves—or perhaps too high an opinion—stooped so low as to demean others through careless words of gossip. Had she not been a victim of such tales?

"No, Your Grace," she said. "It is not that at all." She worried her lip in an effort to form the words to explain. "It is…well, you see…" How *would* she explain?

"Please, you may tell me. I have no reason to ridicule you."

Jane gave a tight sigh. It was just as well he knew. "My eyes, Your Grace. They are of a color that others find…unsettling, perhaps even off-putting. I do not wish for people to stare or speak ill of them."

"Look at me." His voice was kind but held an authoritative tone that Jane did not miss.

Jane did as he bid and looked up at the mass of hair that covered the man's face.

"Your eyes are not terrible," he said after a few moments of study. How he could be sure when he was peering through his hair, she did not know. "They are unique to be sure, but nothing about which to be concerned. Whoever told you that they were off-putting was a fool, and you should not heed their words."

Jane nodded and muttered a thank you as the Duke pulled back his hair to reveal the whole of his face. Scars covered most of the right side, including the entirety of his cheek and jaw, and it was clear that he expected her to react in some negative way. Granted, it was an unsightly scarring, but Jane could see that the man had once been quite handsome, and if one was to study the left cheek, they would see that he still was.

She held his gaze, for she did not wish to upset him by looking away, and she found doing so not as difficult as she would have expected.

"Now, this is not appealing," he said as he pointed to his face. "I have shown you this for I do not like to cover my face. I ask you never to tell anyone about my disfigurement; my name has already been the subject of more rumors than I care to admit."

"Of course, Your Grace," Jane replied, stunned that he would ask such a thing. However, gossip did begin somewhere, and the fact this man did not know her must have been the reasoning for the request. "My time here, however long it shall be, will not be shared with anyone. That much I can promise you. I am here to teach your son and nothing more."

"Well then, Miss Harcourt, I believe we should get that carriage brought around for you. When you return, Jenkins will show you your rooms." He led her to the front of the house. "If you need anything—anything at all—please let me know."

"Thank you, Your Grace. I look forward to my time here." Although she meant every word, she could not help but wonder how a murderer could be so kind.

Chapter Four

When she returned to the cottage belonging to her cousins, Jane set to packing her few belongings. She placed the last item in her bag and slung it over her shoulder. Anne and David stood waiting for her, Anne smoothing her skirts, although they did not need smoothing, and David rubbing together the thumb and forefinger of his right hand as if he wished to remove something sticky from them.

"You must tell us," Anne said, her eyes wide, "is he as horrid as the rumors say? His face...tell me, how hideous was it? I have often wondered..."

Jane let out a small sigh. She owed her cousin much, but the Duke had made it clear his desire to not be the topic of rumor, at least not any more than he already was. Plus, she had given her word.

"I cannot say," she said. When Anne tried to again to ask, she added, "I will tell you this. So far he has been kind to me."

David snorted as if he thought she had contrived a story.

Anne's face dropped in disappointment, but she did not press Jane further, for which Jane was glad. "Be careful of him," she warned. "I heard that his son is as evil as he—a span of Satan as it were." She pulled Jane in for a hug. "Just promise you will be careful," she whispered in Jane's ear.

"There is a darkness around that family," David added. "I don't know why, but it's as if a curse lies on the name." Jane suspected that the man equated speaking the family name with naming the devil himself.

"Do not worry," Jane assured them both. "I know how to handle myself. I must be on my way; the carriage driver must be growing impatient waiting for me."

Anne walked her to the carriage, the sun just above the western horizon punctuating the concern for being on their way. Few ventured the roads in a carriage after dark. Too many had lost their lives when their horse misstepped or a wheel broke due to a hole in the road.

"Thank you," Jane said as she gave Anne one last hug.

"I do worry about you, Love," Anne said when the hug ended. "Please, give me your word that you will be careful."

"My guard is up and my mind is sharp. If I suspect the least bit of trickery, I will return to your home at once."

Anne stroked Jane's hair as if she were sending off her only child. "I know you will, but I cannot help but worry. I wish your mother was alive to see what a beautiful and kind woman you have become. She would be very proud."

Jane smiled, her heart aching still from such a great loss, even after this long. It was Anne and David who had taken her in all those years ago. Their kindness had always been great. "I will visit soon," she promised. Then she picked up her bag and put it in the carriage. With one final hug, she stepped up through the door and sat back into the seat.

The carriage lurched as it moved over the short, rocky drive, and Jane turned to wave at the two people on whom she knew she could count to support her whenever her life became an upheaval. What she would have done without them, she did not know, nor did she wish to know.

When they were out of sight, she once again sat back into the cushioned seat. The road had leveled out and the journey became much smoother. Jane found herself thinking about the man she had met earlier that day, the man better known to the world as the Duke of Fire. The rumors concerning the appearance of his face were true; yet, though the scarring was considerable, Jane had never been one to be frightened by the odd or strange. What she did think on was the fact that the Duke held himself in a much different manner than she had expected. His mannerisms, his voice, both were kind for any man, let alone a man of his standing, which surprised her. It had been her limited experience that the higher the title, the greater the ego, or so her mother had told her. Yet, the man seemed humble, a distinct contradiction to his title.

Then there was Samuel. Although she had only spoken a few words to him, Jane could tell the boy had a great heart. She herself would never have children as she had no hope of ever marrying, but if she could wish for children, she would hope they would be half as kind as he seemed.

The carriage picked up speed, and the sun continued to tuck itself away for the night. Long shadows crept across the road, reaching out to the opposite side. Soon, Jane would be at Wellesley Manor as a resident, and although some of the mysteries of the home had been revealed, she knew many more remained to be discovered.

***

Jane set her brush on the table beside a small hand mirror, the last of her meager possessions, and stepped back to once more look over her new room. Located on the second floor, it was the most beautiful room in which she had ever lived. To her utter amazement, the bed had a large canopy with flowing curtains tied back with ribbon. Although she had never seen it, the servants described such a bed in rooms belonging to the Earl and Countess of Waterwood. Yet she, a simple governess, allowed the opportunity to sleep in such finery was beyond her. And the luxury did not end there. The room also contained a large chest of drawers and a wardrobe so large, she would never fill either. All of the clothes she had ever owned could not have filled them.

She changed into her dressing gown, hanging her day dress in the wardrobe. It looked pitiful hanging beside the two other dresses she owned, not for its quality but rather for the excess space left in the wardrobe. She wondered what it would be like to have so many dresses she had no space to hang another dress. However, she would never be in a position to know what that felt like. Unless she owned the thinnest wardrobe ever made.

With the candle in hand, Jane walked to the window and peered down into the gardens. Although it was already dark, the full moon and shining stars provided enough light for her to see relatively clearly. Tomorrow she planned to take Samuel for a walk to better acquaint her with the boy. Then they would begin their lessons on Monday.

The sound of a voice behind her, though it was quiet, made her almost drop the candle as she swung around. In the doorway stood young Samuel, his face sad.

"I'm sorry, Miss Harcourt," the boy said as he wiped his eyes. "I had a terrible dream."

Jane's heart went out to the boy as she hurried over to him. "I am sorry, Samuel," she said, leaning over to place a hand on his cheek. "I do not like terrible dreams, either. However, we know they are just that— dreams. Do you have good ones, as well?"

This seemed to encourage the boy, for a smile crossed his face. "Oh, yes, I do. May I tell you about one?"

"Yes, you may," Jane said as she straightened. "However, let us return to your room first."

The boy nodded, and she slipped her dressing gown over her nightdress. Then she took his hand and led him back to his room. Of the same size as Jane's, it had a more masculine feel to it. The bed also had a canopy, but the curtains that hung down the sides were a deep blue rather than pale pink as in Jane's room. A dresser held a collection of rocks and other small items more than likely found on past excursions on which Samuel had gone during his short life. How much the room reminded Jane of Arthur Clarkson, her previous young ward.

As Samuel crawled into bed, Jane set the candle on the night table and then leaned in to bring the blanket up to his chin. She sat beside him and smiled when his eyes lit up in anticipation.

"Now, tell me of your good dreams," she said, brushing back the hair that hung over his brow in an unruly fashion.

"I once had a dream that I was riding a horse and rabbits were following me," he said. "There were so many of them, I could not count them."

"Oh, how lovely!" Jane exclaimed. "And where were you taking them?"

"I don't know." He scrunched his brow in thought. "I think it was a place were other rabbits lived so they could play together," he said and then let out a large yawn. "Can you tell me about your dreams?"

Jane smiled at the boy as she thought on her own dreams, though she had not had many as of late, at least not many she could recall.

"When I was your age, I had a dream about finding a box full of gold coins."

This seemed to intrigue the child. "What did you do with it?"

She laughed. "To be honest, I went and bought a beautiful silk blue dress. It was very pretty, though it cost all of the coins in the box. What do you think?"

Samuel grimaced. "I don't like dresses," he said, making Jane laugh.

"I suppose you would not, at that," she said with a tap of her finger on his nose. "Now, you get to sleep and dream about those rabbits," Jane said as she rose from the bed, taking the candle with her. "Perhaps you will learn their destination."

"Miss Harcourt?" His voice was quiet and Jane could hear the sleepiness in it.

"Yes, Samuel?"

"You're not going to leave me like Miss Hester did, are you? It hurt me when she left."

Jane smiled, her heart going out to the child. "No, Samuel," she replied. "At least not for a while." Then she shut the door just as his eyes closed.

As she returned to her room, a noise made her stop and listen and her heart to thump against her chest. It had come from the end of the hall, but she was unable to identify what exactly the sound had been. Her skin went cold and she was unsure what to do. She strained to listen to see if the noise returned, and indeed, it did. It was a voice, muted behind a closed door, a voice that sounded angry.

Jane summoned her courage and tiptoed down the hallway, the candle casting her shadow against the wall. Then another cry made her jump, and she paused to listen again. Her hand trembled and the shadows moved at strange angles, but she continued her trek, stopping before what she understood to be the door that led to the rooms belonging to the Duke. Again, she listened into the dark but the voice did not return.

Chastising herself for a fool, she turned and started back toward her rooms. Who was she to be walking through the hallways of the home of a Duke, especially on her first day in residence?

"Oh, Elizabeth." This time the voice was clearer and came from inside the room on the other side of the door where she currently stood—the

Duke's bedroom. Jane knew that the Duke's wife, who had died in the fire Anne had mentioned, was named Elizabeth, and she wondered if she was the woman to which the Duke now referred. And why was he calling out her name?

Although Jane should have returned to her room, she chose to stay. Moving closer, she leaned her ear toward the door and held her breath, waiting to see of the man repeated his previous words. Her heart pounded behind her ears and she held her breath as she listened in the silence around her. Then the Duke spoke again.

"Elizabeth, I am sorry for what I did."

***

When she returned to her room, Jane sat in bed, the pillows propped up behind her. She should have been asleep, but she found it difficult to do so. By all accounts, the Duke had killed his wife, but she had refused to believe it. If he had, he would have been prosecuted and sentenced to death; even a Duke could not get away with such an act. However, he had confessed as much in his sleep, and she wondered what she should do about it. Perhaps there had been insufficient evidence to convict him, yet if the magistrates had his confession, would they then prosecute?

Her eyes darted to the door. Would the man realize that she had overheard him and come to her room to murder her? Or would he choose to simply take out his anger and guilt on the governess? Those thoughts led her to wonder why the previous governess left the position. Had she been forced to leave because she feared for her life?

Closing her eyes for a moment, she tried to remain calm and explore her options. She could slip away now, or in the morning, and return to Anne's, but the thought of intruding on her cousin's life once again made her stomach ache. She did not wish to become a burden to anyone, even someone who had given her so much already, no matter how bleak her current situation appeared.

When she opened her eyes, she felt a bit more relaxed and the panic had subsided considerably. Perhaps the Duke was truly sorry for what he did, thus the confession. Or maybe what had happened had been an accident after all.

This conundrum intrigued Jane for some odd reason. She knew all too well that rumors oftentimes were untrue. The Duke could have easily started the fire by mishap, which would explain both his facial scars as well as the guilt he felt.

Feeling much better, she leaned over and blew out the candle. Then she slid down into the bed and pulled the covers up to her chin. She had made a decision to remain at Wellesley Manor, but she would remain vigilant, keeping her eyes and ears alert. A smile came to her face as her eyelids grew heavy, and within minutes sleep overtook her.

Chapter Five

E lizabeth, I am sorry for what I did."

Michael sat up straight in bed, clutching at his chest in an attempt to keep his heart within the confines of his sternum. His breathing was ragged and he was covered in a fine sheen of sweat. Tears stung his eyes, the pain of the memories of that fateful night still eating away at him. How long would these dreams continue? he wondered.

The sound of a floorboard groaning in the hallway caught his attention, and he noticed a weak light leaking under the door. Perhaps Jenkins was moving about the house as he was wont to do, or one of the scullery maids was about her business before the household awoke. It could be any number of scenarios, but Michael would not allow his imagination to run wild.

Rising from the bed, he went and threw open the window to allow the night air to cool the room and his skin. Although the nightmare had ended, the guilt remained in its stead as it always did. No matter how much money he earned or the love he had for his son, his conscience was never cleared. At one point in his life, he had not been a madman. As a matter of fact, quite the opposite was the case. He had fallen in love with Elizabeth and their wedding had been a grand affair, rivaling even that of the Prince himself. His wife had been a gracious and kind woman to everyone she encountered, a light that gave him strength even in his darkest times. Then, before he knew it, Samuel had come into their lives bringing them a joy neither had ever known, and happiness surrounded them at every turn.

However, that light Elizabeth emanated had been snuffed out that fateful night, and his strength, his love, was gone forever, leaving behind a motherless child and a husband who had become the husk of the man he once was.

Shaking his head to rid himself of the thoughts, he walked over to a stand that held a pitcher of water. He poured himself a glass, splashed what remained into the matching bowl, and then washed away as much of the sweat as he could. Skin pebbles dotted his arms, and he shivered. Drinking of the cool liquid rewarded his parched throat.

He returned to his bed and lay on top of the covers, his thoughts going to the new woman in the house, Miss Harcourt. She was beautiful, far more beautiful than most women he had encountered in his life. Yet, she was unaware of her beauty, her silky brown hair, her clear, gray eyes. To his astonishment, she was ashamed of those eyes, the eyes that, when he gazed into them, brought forth a feeling he had not experienced for many years—not since before losing Elizabeth.

Then there was the woman's spirit. The immediate liking she took to Samuel was much too authentic to have been staged, and Samuel had seemed to take her just as easily, which pleased Michael no end. For Samuel's happiness was of the utmost importance, and he would do anything to protect the boy from harm.

For a moment, he considered what it would be like to hold the dark-haired beauty in his arms. To press his lips to hers as he tightened his embrace. Then he shook his head. He was Master of this house, and it was not right for him to look at a servant—be she scullery maid or governess—in such a way. While other men looked upon those of lower class as property, Michael could do no such thing. To him, even servants deserved to be treated fairly, and that meant not thinking of them as something other than real people who happen to be in his employ.

Letting out a sigh, he brought his hand to his face and caressed the scars that disfigured his once-handsome features. Besides the madness that grew stronger every week, his face was such that no woman would wish to marry him, at least not for love. Plenty of women would endure his presence to obtain the title of Duchess and to dig into his deep coffers. However, he would rather live alone than to share a bed with a woman whose heart was closed to him, a woman who chose to use him for what he could give her monetarily and socially.

None of that mattered, for there were more important things to consider at the moment. His first priority was Samuel's education and watching the boy become a man. What Michael wanted above all else was that Samuel became a man of integrity, a man who was honest and forthright, and a man with a strong sense of right and wrong. That would be followed by a great understanding of business so he would be able to continue the legacy that had been passed down to him.

Despite these goals, Michael's greatest fears remained. Would he be sane enough to witness his son reaching greatness, or would the madness that threatened him at every turn take him completely before then?

***

Saturday afternoon, Miss Harcourt was in the garden with Samuel. The boy's lessons would not begin for another two days, and the woman had insisted that she use the time until then to get to know the boy. Michael had thought the idea wonderful; what other governess would take such time to become acquainted with her ward when she could simply take her leisure until the studies were to begin?

"I must ask, my dear brother. Why would employ a governess who has no references for the past year?" Robert asked as the two sat in the drawing room.

Michael turned and studied the man beside him. Unlike Michael, Robert had light hair and eyes, having inherited their mother's features. Beneath the fine cut of his coat were a mass of well-defined muscles which Michael envied, for it meant that Robert had more opportunities to be outside, working those muscles—although not as much as those in his employ—while Michael spent his days indoors, the majority of his days spent at his desk working numbers and entering information into his ledgers. It was not that he did not enjoy his work, for he did, but he wished he could be more involved with the day-to-day workings of the business like his brother was.

Robert was not finished with his assessment of the new governess. "Surely you understand that she was more than likely doing far more than educating children."

41

Michael knew his brother meant well, for he cared very much for Samuel and had always had the boy's best interests at heart; however, the man spoke his mind all too freely as far as Michael was concerned.

"I see you have purchased another fine coat," Michael said in an attempt to change the subject. Although he rarely left the house, he was no stranger to the latest fashions, and what Robert wore this day was most definitely new.

Robert looked down. "Oh, yes, I do allow myself fine clothes from time to time," he replied, his voice carrying a note of humility that his eyes did not show. "Now, concerning this woman. Do you trust her?"

This made Michael laugh. "As much as I can trust anyone I allow in my home, I suppose. I care not why she left Henry Clarkson's employ, but I would assume the man's hands still wander where his eyes have been?"

Robert snorted. "You speak no lie, Brother, for Clarkson has been known to bed more women than I dare count." He took a sip of his brandy and set the glass on the table. "Michael, I worry about you. I know at times it seems I ridicule our decisions, but I am only trying to be sure you and Samuel are safe...from those who mean to do you harm."

Michael considered his brother's words. "Who would wish to do me harm?"

The man's eyes wandered to the large window that overlooked the gardens. "Take the woman out there with Samuel at this moment," he said, pointing with a jut to his chin. "As an example, not the woman in particular."

"Very well, then."

"A person such as she would love nothing more than to find solace in her life, but it would not be in your arms but in your coffers." Robert placed a hand on Michael's arm. "I realize the pain you feel over the loss of Elizabeth." Michael winced, not from the man's touch but from his words, and Robert removed his hand. "I only pray you are careful." He let out a small sigh and lowered his head.

Michael took a drink of his own brandy and thought about his brother's words. His brother was right. Michael had thought often about the type of people Robert mentioned, and he knew the risks of bringing someone as beautiful as Miss Harcourt into his home, but the pool had been shallow, at least for someone with the history of the Duke of Fire, and beggars could not be choosers, or so the saying went.

At least he had his brother to look out for him, and for that he was grateful. The man had a heart of kindness and always had Michael's, as well as Samuel's, best interests in mind. If it had not been for him, always beside Michael and never once complaining, Michael knew not where he would be today.

"I have no concerns when it comes to Miss Harcourt," Michael said finally. "She is a kind woman. The fire did not take away my judgment of people. However, I do appreciate not only your wisdom this day, but everything you have done for me."

Robert rose from his seat, his drink in hand. He walked to the window and looked out into the garden. "Good," he replied. "I know your judgment is sound." He sipped his brandy, never taking his eyes off the garden. "How has your mind been as of late?" he asked.

The question caught Michael off-guard, though he had suspected it would come soon enough. "The nightmares continue to plague me, and the guilt of that night is still fresh." He shook his head. "I wonder if it will ever leave me. Then I worry…"

Robert turned toward Michael. "Worry about what?"

Michael shrugged. If it had been anyone other than Robert, he would not have answered, but this was his brother, the man who cared for him despite his face, and his mind. "My mind. I fear it is worsening. Just yesterday, I came here to the drawing room to find Elizabeth's pillow, the one I would take in my carriage. I always returned it to that chair." He pointed to the chair Elizabeth had favored before her death. "However, yesterday it was in the far corner on the floor. I would never leave Elizabeth's pillow on the floor." Shame and sickness overwhelmed him.

His brother walked over and knelt down beside him. "Guilt can cause the nightmares, so that can be answered quite easily." He placed a hand once again on Michael's arm. "However, I hate to say this, but it can also produce the bouts of madness you are showing."

The words pained Michael. "It plagues me, for I fear I will go mad before Samuel comes of age. I worry about his future. If I lose my senses too early, what will become of him?" He downed the measure of brandy remaining in his glass in one gulp, the fiery liquid relieving his pain, albeit temporarily.

Robert stood and poured himself another brandy. "I must admit that I worry watching you slowly deteriorate. I have already spoken to Catherine concerning this matter."

This caused Michael to gasp. "Surely you did not..."

However, Robert did not allow him to finish. "No, I did not tell her of your troubles exactly; you know me far better than that." He placed a hand on Michael's shoulder. "I merely asked her, if anything was to happen to my brother, what would become of Samuel? Her response made me the proudest man in England."

Michael looked up at his brother. "What was her response?"

"That we would raise the boy as our own and that she would stop at nothing to make sure the boy was happy." Robert returned to his chair and placed his hands on his knees. "We are to have our own children one day, but she even said that she wishes they would be as wonderful as Samuel. Her words, not mine."

Michael smiled. What his brother said soothed his worries. If he did go mad, which he no doubt would eventually, at least Samuel would be left in good hands, with family he could trust.

"I am sorry I was unable to attend your wedding," Michael said. Robert and his wife had married only two weeks earlier, but anxiety and fear had kept Michael from attending. The thought of people staring at him on such an important day made him decline his brother's invitation, although it truly did make him sad that his illness kept him from attending such important functions.

"As I have told you many times, it was not your fault. We knew you were with us in spirit. Let us speak no more of it." He rose and went to refill Michael's glass. "Now, you relax; you are much too agitated. It cannot be good for your current state of mind." When he returned the decanter to the cart, he turned to walk toward the door. "I believe I will go speak to my nephew before I leave. Unless you need me to stay longer."

"No, I feel much better, thank you."

"Good. I will leave you to it."

As he placed his hand on the door handle, Michael said, "Robert?"

Robert turned back to Michael. "Yes?"

"Thank you for all you have done—and continue to do—for myself and Samuel."

"But of course," Robert replied with a wide grin. "I would not have it any other way."

Chapter Six

The blue sky was filled with white, fluffy clouds. Birds sang their joyous song from the branches that hung overhead. A slight breeze helped cool the air heated by the sun above. All these things made for a wonderful afternoon as Jane learned about Samuel.

However, despite the loveliness of the day, the words she overheard the previous night still plagued her mind. She had hurried back to her own room, the sound of floorboards creaking beneath her small feet echoing off the walls, or so it seemed in the otherwise silence that surrounded her. She had imagined the Duke chasing her down the hall and, once he caught her, setting her on fire. Thoughts products of her wild imagination, to be sure, but there nonetheless.

By the time she had rushed into her room and closed the door behind her, the conjecture fled, replaced by rational thought. The Duke would gain nothing by killing her, and he would only draw more attention to himself if she were to go missing, or worse, be found dead.

She smiled as she thought of Anne. If anything happened to Jane, Anne would break down the doors of Wellesley Manor in search of the person who had wronged her. Yes, although the Duke might be a murderer, Jane knew she was safe. At least for now.

"Do you think rabbits understand what we say?" Samuel asked, breaking Jane from her thoughts. The boy was playing with a long stem of grass, rolling it between his fingers as he scrunched his brow.

"To be honest, I do not know," Jane answered. When she saw the disappointment on the boy's face, she quickly added, "But I believe that all animals do hear us." She gave Samuel a smile as she smoothed her skirts that rested on the blanket on which the two sat.

"Oh, that is brilliant," Samuel said in awe. "I talk to birds sometimes." He threw the blade of grass away from him. "Sometimes they talk back to me."

"Is that so?" Jane asked with amusement. "And what do they say?"

"They say, 'Samuel, you are such a good boy.'" The boy gave her an endearing grin that made her laugh until she cried.

"Well, although I have not known you very long," she said as she wiped away tears, "I believe you are a very good boy, as well."

His smile practically split his face in two. "Thank you," he replied. "And although I have only known you a short time, I find you a very nice woman. Not like Miss Pambury." He grimaced as he said the name and shook his head.

"Now, Samuel," Jane admonished lightly, imagining that he was speaking of a former governess, "we do not speak ill of other people when they are not here to defend themselves, and you especially should not speak ill of women. It is not becoming of a young man such as yourself to speak so."

The boy sighed. "I know. She's just mean, and I don't like her. She doesn't like children much either." Jane went to speak, but he continued before she could say a word. "She's always mean to me when father is not around."

Jane cleared her throat, unsure of whom Samuel spoke. The woman could not have been a previous governess if he spoke of her as if she still came around. However, regardless of who this Miss Pambury was, Jane refused to allow the boy to participate in idle gossip.

"Are you still interested in exploring the gardens?" she asked to take his mind off this unknown woman.

He nodded and pulled himself up from the blanket. "I'm going to find my rabbit friends," he said with a wide grin. "Should I look for gold coins so you can buy a new dress?"

Jane smiled at the boy. His heart was made of the gold he wished to find. "Yes, please," she replied.

With that, he ran off, leaving Jane to gather the picnic lunch, or what was left of it, and the blanket. Her plan had been to ease Samuel's mind

47

so he would feel free to share with her where he left off in his schooling with Miss Hester and to determine what he knew thus far. As it turned out, he was a bright boy, although this did not surprise her. He had a wonderful wit about him and his avid tendency for curiosity showed her that he could pick up just about anything—as long as it interested him. Overall, she looked forward to beginning his instruction come Monday.

Jane watched the boy as he walked around the corner of the house and out of sight. As she went to stand, the temperature seemed to drop and a shadow fell over her.

"The boy has taken a liking to you," a man's voice said from behind her.

Jane turned. She did not recognize the man who stood before her, but he had similar features to the Duke, although his hair was shorter with a lighter hue, and he was not as handsome somehow.

"Please, allow me to assist you," the man said as he held out a hand.

She took the offered hand and pulled herself to a standing position before she gave him a curtsy as she looked at the man's shoes. "Thank you, My Lord. My name is Miss Jane…"

"Yes, I know who you are," the man said as he cut her off. "Please, look at me when I speak to you." Although the words were almost the same as those spoken by the Duke, this man's tone was not as soft.

Jane forced herself to bring her eyes to his face.

"What beautiful eyes you have," he said in a low voice. Then he cleared his throat. "Allow me to introduce myself. I am Robert Blackstone, younger brother of Michael Blackstone, your employer."

Jane offered a return smile and tried to hold the man's gaze. It was not that he was less polite than the Duke, but something about him said he did not share the Duke's soft countenance but instead preferred to use a more authoritative approach when dealing with servants.

"I wish to speak to you, if you will. Follow me."

Swallowing hard, Jane did as he bade, leaving the remains of the picnic lunch where they lay. She could easily return for them later.

"I told my brother it was unwise to have you reside here while you watched over his son," Lord Blackstone said. "Although he claims you are a kind person and there is nothing to fear, I must be certain that this is the case." They came to a stop before a small birdbath and he turned to look at her. "Tell me, is there anything about which I should worry while you look after my nephew?"

"No, My Lord," Jane replied in surprise. "I will instruct him with the best of my ability to ensure his education is the best he can receive."

The man nodded, and Jane lowered her eyes. The uneasiness had returned, and she found it difficult to hold the man's gaze.

"Very well, then," Lord Blackstone said with finality, as if she had somehow just passed some sort of test. "I will take you at your word, even if you are a woman. However, I will ask one thing from you, and I hope you will assist me with it."

"Of course, My lord," she replied and then immediately regretted the words. Why would she agree to something before she knew the terms of that agreement? For some reason, her uneasiness with this man increased.

"My brother is suffering greatly from the tragedy of losing his wife and the mother to his son. His mind has not been his own since, and I am afraid that he only worsens as time goes by."

Jane gave a single nod, her memories of the previous night coming to her. His brother spoke the truth.

"He grows angrier and more confused each day. What he remembers now, he forgets in an hour. What I am asking is this." He brought his fingers to her chin and lifted her face to look at her directly. Her skin prickled at his touch. "If you see or hear anything that causes you worry, will you inform me? My brother and his son are all I have left in this world. If anything were to happen to him, or if the madness overtakes him to the point he is unable to perform his duties necessary to his title, it will crush me. Promise me you will report at once anything out of the ordinary."

Jane nodded again, this time with more vigor. Perhaps the coldness in his eyes came from the pain he felt for what was happening with his brother. Maybe she had misjudged him.

"Thank you," he said as he released her chin and gave her a smile. "The relief knowing you are here and watching eases my mind greatly."

"Of course, My Lord," she said with a curtsy. "However I can help, I will."

Lord Blackstone smiled again and, without another word, headed back toward the house.

Jane wiped at her chin before she realized she did so, as if to rid herself of the memory of his touch. His words worked through her mind. If the Duke was going mad as his brother said, it would explain the words about his wife she overheard the previous night. However, she could not shake the confusion within her as she walked off in search of Samuel. If this man cared so deeply for his brother, why did he leave a bad taste in her mouth?

***

"Splendid," Jane said as Samuel finished writing out yet another sentence. For their first day of instruction, they had completed quite a few lessons, for the boy was more than competent, even at his young age.

Samuel looked up at her and smiled before returning the quill to its holder. "Miss Hester told me I am very smart," he said as a statement of fact.

Jane returned his smile as she rubbed his mop of dark hair. "I believe Miss Hester was correct in her observation," she said truthfully. "You are a very bright boy. Now, are you ready to show me your skills in reading?"

"Oh, yes," he replied with a ready grin. "But might we go outside to read? It's too nice to be inside today."

Jane laughed and looked out the large window. "I do believe you make a very good point," she said. "Very well, we will go outside. However, we will be there to read. No chasing rabbits or looking for gold coins while completing lessons."

"Yes, Miss Harcourt," Samuel answered, although he sounded a bit disappointed.

Taking the boy's hand in hers, the two left the study, passing Jenkins, who gave a polite smile. The butler was rigid, but Jane sensed a kindness about the man. Perhaps after some time he would be less former toward her.

Soon the pair were outside and Samuel chose a bench under a large birch tree. Storm clouds brewed along the horizon, already bringing about a coolness to the air, but for the time being, the sun shone brightly on them.

"Now, Samuel," Jane said as she opened a book she had brought out with her, "I would like you to read to me." She handed him the book, which he took with a soberness that made her hide a smile. He did take his lessons quite seriously indeed.

"There was…once a man who…" He looked up at her. "What's that word?"

"Sought."

"There was…once a man who sought to find…"

Jane listened as the boy called out the words on the page, and although he struggled with some, she was overall impressed at his reading ability. The majority of the words over which he stumbled would have been difficult for any reader his age, but the majority he read perfectly.

"Did Miss Hester read with you every day?" she asked a short time later when she asked him to discontinue his reading.

The boy shook his head.

"Once a week?" she asked, finding it odd that the woman would not have found reading on a daily basis an important part of his education.

"Just two times," he said in reply, raising two fingers to punctuate his answer. "She would give me a book and then sometimes she would fall asleep."

Jane smiled, the problem now apparent. "Well, from now on, you will read every day. How does that sound?"

He gave her a skeptical look. "I like that, but will I still be able to play?"

She laughed. "Of course," she said. "Go on and play now before we get you ready for dinner."

Without hesitating even a moment, Samuel jumped up from the bench and took off down the nearby steps. Jane let out a sigh and then turned, her eyes widening when she saw the Duke walking toward her with long strides. His long hair flowed behind him, and the dark storm clouds provided a perfect backdrop for his scarred face. Her heart raged, for she feared he was somehow enraged at her.

"Miss Harcourt," he said as he stopped before her. "May I join you?"

Jane swallowed hard and tried to regain her senses, hoping her fear would subside. The Duke, however, tilted his head as she struggled to speak, so she gave him a quick nod in reply. Rather than being angry with her, however, he simply took a seat beside her. Her heartbeat quickened; she had never been so close to a murderer before.

"What is your assessment of Samuel?" he asked in a kind voice that belied the grimace on his face.

Jane grasped the book so hard as a means to hold onto something her fingers pained her.

"Miss Harcourt? Are you well?"

Something inside her clicked and she realized that she was acting the fool. A quick study of his face made her realize that the grimace she thought he wore was, in fact, a permanent expression he carried due to the extensive scarring. What a fool she was.

"I apologize, Your Grace," she said when she had released the tight grip on the book. "In answer to your question, Samuel is an exceptional student with a mind that is eager to learn. His skills in mathematics are higher than others his age with whom I've worked, and I believe his reading skills will improve with practice."

It was quiet for a few moments, and Jane allowed a glance over at the Duke. Was he angry or upset at the news? Did it displease him that she had not included reading as an exceptional skill the boy possessed? She refused to lie about what the boy could and could not do; in doing so, it only hurt the student rather than helped. Granted, it made the parents feel better, but it did no good for the child.

Her fear eased, however, when the man looked at her, and though she could not see his eyes, for he had pulled his hair back over his face, she could feel them on her.

"It is good to know how well he is doing. An education is of great importance for the role he will one day inherit, and although he will more than likely attend a boarding school as well as University, the foundation he builds today will only make him a greater success later."

"I would agree wholeheartedly," Jane said. "To walk in his father's footsteps will be a great task, and I will make sure he is ready to the best of my skills." She paused for a moment as she returned her gaze to the ground. Her cheeks had heated significantly. "Forgive me for being so forward, Your Grace," she said when she realized she might have overstepped her place. "I did not mean to imply that I could ever understand the importance of your station."

The laugh the Duke gave was not menacing, which is what Jane had expected, but instead held mirth. "You are very kind, Miss Harcourt," he said, "and I understand the intentions of your words. They were not presumptuous but rather came from the heart."

Jane gave him a shy smile. Murderer or not, he did seem kind, and his laugh had a way of making her relax in his presence. Daring to sneak a peek, she raised her head once more and her eyes met his.

He wore a smile and his cheeks had a pink hue to them. "You are a welcome addition to my home. I had feared that I would not find anyone." He rose from the bench. "To be honest, I thought I would have to settle for a governess no one else wanted." Although he loomed above her, she found she no longer feared him for some reason. "Although it seems that my fears were for naught. It seems that I have acquired the most brilliant mind to instruct my son."

The compliment warmed Jane's heart—and her cheeks. "Thank you, Your Grace," she said. "Your words are very kind."

"I do not say so to be kind. I simply wish to be honest." His smile widened. "I would request that you join us for dinner tonight. It has become lonesome when it is just Samuel and me dining alone, and he would certainly welcome your presence."

Jane sat in stunned silence. The Earl of Waterwood had insisted that Jane eat with Arthur—or perhaps it was the Countess who insisted. Regardless, in every position she had held, as the governess, she was never invited to eat with the family, and to be asked to do so was a windfall indeed. What an honor it would be to sit at the same table as a Duke.

"I will graciously accept your offer,"

"I will see you at six in the dining room," the Duke said in a tone that brooked no argument. "If you would like to retire for a short while, I will find Samuel and bring him in." Without waiting for her answer, he walked away as thunder rumbled in the distance.

A new thought occurred to Jane. How could the Duke of Fire, a suspected murderer, make her feel at ease while his brother, a man who appeared kind and giving, cause her to tremble in fear? If the stories were true, the opposite should have been true. However, as she made her way back to the house, she knew it mattered not at this moment. For now, she needed to prepare herself for dinner with the Duke of Fire. As the storm above her started to close in, she wondered if it was an omen as to what was to come.

***

The idea of dining with the Duke still held a bit of strangeness—and excitement. Jane looked herself over in the mirror one last time and smiled. Her hair had been pinned up and tied with a ribbon of blue, thick strands of curls allowed to fall on either side of her face. Although she did not typically think herself beautiful, the blue dress she wore—the finest she had ever owned—had her reconsider the notion. Although it was unlikely that anyone of the *ton* would take notice of her dress, even if it was made of silk, for some unknown reason the thought of the Duke doing so had her shaking, and not in the same way she had done so in the presence of his brother. Now her trembling was a pleasant feeling, one built on some sort of hope. What hope she could possibly desire to fill, she was uncertain, but it was there nonetheless.

However, when her eyes greeted her, they seemed to mock her, and she quickly looked down at her gloved hands. How could any man see her beautiful with eyes such as hers?

Letting out a sigh, she released the hope that had been on her heart. Now, she only wished that the Duke would find her dress appropriate and that he enjoyed her company. She did have her wits after all.

She made her way to the dining room, and as she passed a large clock, she was pleased to see she was early. Even her father had insisted on punctuality when it came to dinner, and he was not even a member of the gentry. However, he did find the notion of his family at the table sharing in a meal as important. In his opinion, if a person arrived late to dinner, that person was an uncouth fool. Well, she would be no such person to make such a horrible impression by being late to her first dinner with the Duke, a man she had a great desire to impress, even if it was by her punctual arrival to the dinner table.

When she stepped into the dining room, she smiled at the large table finely decorated with lovely table settings at one end, the Duke in the place of honor at the head and young Samuel to his right. The final setting was across from Samuel, to the Duke's left. When the two took note of her entrance, they rose, and a footman pulled out the chair for her.

"Miss Harcourt," the Duke said with a smile, or a half-smile, as the scars made such an action difficult, "we are glad to have you join us this evening."

"Yes, Miss Harcourt," Samuel said, his smile wide, "you look pretty in that dress. Did you buy it with the gold coins I found?" At least the boy made a comment on her attire; his father certainly had not. She admonished herself for thinking such things; impressing the Duke was not the reason she was here, at least not the main reason.

The Duke gave his son a light reprimand. "Now, Samuel, we do not discuss the price of a woman's dress within her hearing, nor do we ask how she paid for it. It is rude."

Samuel looked down at the table, but his smile did not leave his face. "Yes, Father."

Jane smiled. Father and son clearly had a loving relationship or Samuel would have been far from smiling when his father corrected him. "Thank you both for allowing me this honor," she said as she took her seat, the footman pushing in the chair. "And Samuel, I bought this dress with coins, but I must admit they were not gold coins." She glanced at the Duke, hoping she had not overstepped her bounds by discussing a topic he had deemed unacceptable, but rather than be angry, he appeared amused.

Samuel, however, appeared disappointed. "Well, then the next dress you purchase should be done so with gold." He said this with determination and finality, and Jane had to hide her widening smile behind her hand.

The first course arrived, a creamy soup Jane enjoyed immensely.

"Well, Miss Harcourt, how are you finding your first days here at

Wellesley Manor? I hope your rooms are to your liking."

Jane set her spoon on the side of the bowl. "Oh, yes, very much so. I have never had a room so extravagant before."

This surprised the Duke. "I am glad to hear that yours is so agreeable," he replied. "And your first day with Samuel? Did that go well?"

"Most definitely," she said, flashing a smile at the boy in question. "He is bright, imaginative, and eager—exactly what a governess would want in a ward."

Samuel beamed at the compliment.

"And you, Samuel, do you find Miss Harcourt satisfactory?"

Samuel nodded emphatically. "Most definitely," he replied with a firm tone. "I think she's quite wonderful."

Jane could feel her cheeks warm. "I believe we will learn much while I am with you," she said.

The boy gave her a quizzical look. "While you are with me? Are you wanting to leave soon? I hope not because we have so many things to learn and do."

"I plan to be here as long as your father will allow," Jane said, pleased by the young man's high interest in learning. He truly did have an inquisitive mind, and she hoped to be with him for as long as possible.

The footman came to remove the remains of the first course and others took his place, trays of various dishes in hand. Venison with sweet preserves, boiled potatoes with butter, peas, and sliced bread. It was a veritable feast, and much more than Jane hoped to eat. She hoped her sleep was not interrupted by an upset stomach after eating too much food.

The meal continued with light conversation, and Jane found herself enjoying the company of such fine people. Not fine in the sense that the family was titled, but rather that the members of said family were pleasant conversationalists. She filed each topic of interest Samuel discussed so she could build on them during her instruction. Most included the typical subjects of toads and insects—the later cut short by the Duke explaining that such discussion was not appropriate for the dinner table—and other topics about which she knew little but to which she hoped she could find reference. She had always been very resourceful when it came to researching information for her wards.

By the end of the meal, Jane felt she had learned much about the man who was her employer and his son. She also began to doubt the legitimacy of the rumors she had heard about the Duke and his late wife. How could a man so kind and caring hurt another human being, especially the woman he loved?

However, Jane also knew that many men were capable of hiding the deepest, darkest of secrets. Was this man one of them?

She shook the question from her head. Tonight was meant for enjoyment, not speculation. However, she knew she would keep vigilant regardless of how well this evening went, for her very life might depend on it.

Chapter Seven

A week had passed since the lovely dinner with the Duke, and now coming to the end of her second week at Wellesley Manor, Jane found herself enjoying her new position more than she could have imagined. Samuel was a wonderful learner, and she was pleased with his attention to her instruction. However, although she enjoyed the boy's company, she found herself missing the company of other adults, for after that single dinner with the Duke and Samuel, she had not been invited back to their table. Not that she had expected it, per se, for a governess did not share a table with her employer, but knowing how much she enjoyed their conversation made her miss it all the more.

The other servants in the house were cordial, but no one had the time—or the desire—to converse with her. She understood that her position as governess set her apart from the rest of the servants, but she also was not a member of the family, thus she was somewhere in between the two. It had been the same with her previous employer. Yet, at least there being alone when she was not tending young Arthur had been a reprieve from the roaming eyes of Lord Clarkson.

Perhaps in a few days she would be allowed a day to visit her cousin Anne. It would be wonderful to spend the day with her and to enjoy her company.

"Miss Harcourt," Samuel said, pulling Jane from her thoughts. She pulled the covers up to his chin, "are you going to kiss me goodnight?"

Jane smiled and leaned over to place a light kiss on the boy's forehead. "Have a good night's sleep and dream of rabbits for me," she said.

The boy smiled, his eyelids heavy as he fought to keep them open. Inquisitive children oftentimes refused to sleep, and Samuel was no exception. "I will try to catch one for you," he said and then yawned deeply.

Jane stood and turned toward the door, and her heart leapt into her throat when she saw the Duke leaning against the door frame. He said nothing as he stepped aside to allow Jane to pass.

Once the door was closed behind them, he turned toward her. "The sun has not yet set," he said. Did he sound nervous? "I would like to take a stroll around the gardens and would enjoy it if you accompanied me. I must admit that, outside of a few business acquaintances, I have little opportunity for conversation with others."

Had the man listened in on her thoughts? Jane wondered. She racked her brain in an attempt to recall if she had somehow murmured her thoughts aloud, but if she had, Samuel would have commented. She gave him a nod, and without another word, they made their way through the house and stepped onto the veranda into the cool night air. As he had said, the sun had yet to set, though it would not be long before it did so and night befell them.

"I hope you are settling in well in my home," the Duke said as they began to stroll down the cobbled path.

"Yes, Your Grace," Jane replied. "I have found everything to my liking and much more."

He made no further comment as they came to a place where the path split, and they stopped before a large hedge as he seemed to consider in which direction to turn.

"We will go this way," he said finally, turning left, away from the house.

Jane looked ahead as they walked, the boughs of the large trees on either side of the path now blocking the majority of the remaining light. For a moment, the thought of him attacking her for some reason known only to him made her feel frightened, but then she took a deep breath to regain her composure. The man had not given her reason to even consider such silly thoughts and by all accounts seemed kind enough to trust.

"You do not say much, Miss Harcourt," he said. "Have I done anything to upset you?"

"No, not at all, Your Grace," Jane replied, guilt for thinking such horrible thoughts about the man abounding. "I...well, I know my place and would never presume to speak out of turn..."

He stopped and stared at her. "Your social standing has nothing to do with us conversing when we are alone. Please, speak freely to me as though we are well-acquainted friends."

Jane nodded. This was uncommon. No, unbelievable. No one she had known who was of the Nobility had ever offered her this privilege. "Very well, then," she replied, surprised that her voice was not shaking. She attempted to come up with a topic safe enough for social conversation. "I look forward to cooler days soon. The temperature has been unbearable as of late."

They came to the end of the path and a large field lay before them just on the other side of a low stone wall. The field appeared to roll out and touch the horizon in the distance where the sun peeked out for one final look over the land.

"I could not agree with you more," the Duke said. "Soon, winter will return, and another year will have passed." His voice sounded strained and Jane wondered as to why. "Tell me something, Miss Harcourt. Do you find me the person I have been made out to be?"

His question caught her off-guard, and Jane was uncertain as to how to respond. If she answered in the negative, then she would be admitting she knew of the rumors concerning him and the death of his wife. If she played ignorant, he would not believe her.

The Duke seemed to sense her inner battle to reply and turned to face her, and she immediately looked to the ground. "Miss Harcourt," he said, his voice as soft as silk, "a woman of your beauty should hold her head up high, no matter who she stands before."

Jane raised her head and looked at the man. "Thank you, Your Grace, for your kind words."

"Now, please, do you find me as evil as the rumors say?"

Jane looked into the Duke's eyes and for the first time saw the pain they held. Why would a man of his title and wealth concern himself with the wagging tongues of others? However, high or low, all men and women concerned themselves with how others perceived them. In her heart, she knew she should tell him the truth.

"I have found that your words and actions are quite the opposite from the rumors I have heard. I do not say that to retain my position here; it is simply the truth."

The Duke let out a laugh as he pushed his long hair over his shoulder. "Finally, I have found someone who speaks the truth to me. Jenkins has been with me for many years and is my most loyal servant. However, he denies ever hearing rumors about me. Thank you for your honesty, for only a friend would be so honest."

Jane smiled, although she was not certain why. Inside she regretted her truthfulness and she was surprised how well the man took the news that rumors did exist. Yet, she knew that, regardless of a person's station, tongues wagged and people gossiped, and although some did not share in passing along hurtful words, all too many did.

The Duke turned his gaze back to the field, and Jane followed suit. "I often wonder what would happen if I were to make an appearance in the town," he said as if he were speaking aloud to himself. "Would others come to find me half the beast they think I am? However, the shame I feel is much too great, and just as Robert has explained to me, it is best if I remain here. It would be best for myself and for Samuel if those wagging tongues were given no more ammunition."

Jane glanced over and saw the look of hurt on his face, and a strange thing happened to her. Her heart went out to the man, a feeling of sadness for that pain. For all her words of how speaking of others was terrible, she had to admit that she had participated in gossip on more than one occasion but had never truly seen the effects of it. Although her position was to teach his son, a new obligation came to mind, a way to make right any rumors she had helped spread, even if they had not necessarily concerned him.

"Your Grace," she began carefully, "how long has it been since you left your lands?"

More of the sun disappeared, leaving just a pink haze in its wake, and he gave a heavy sigh. "Nearly six years. After Elizabeth…" He closed his eyes and took a deep breath. "When I moved to this estate five years ago was the last time I left."

Jane was shocked. "That is far too long for anyone to be confined to one place," she said, attempting to keep admonishment from her tone. Who was she to admonish a Duke? Friend or no, she still knew her place. "You must leave these grounds and begin to make your presence known to one and all. Put everyone at ease and dispel the rumors of who you truly are."

"Your words are kind, Miss Harcourt, but there is a problem," he said as he turned back to her, the last rays of light casting on his face. "My face would scare both woman and child and would only fuel the rumors about me. Right now, there is a question of how badly I was burned, but once they beheld the truth, they would see that I look far worse than they could ever imagine." He shook his head dejectedly. "No, I am afraid they would only run and hide as soon as I arrived."

"Perhaps," she said. "However, just like my eyes and the ridicule that haunts me, I had to make a choice."

"And what was that?"

"To live in fear or face it," she stated firmly. "Let those who wish to speak ill of you to do so to your face. They will speak so just the same, for that is all they know. Let those who hide behind their false smiles utter their words of contempt in the open!" Her heart was beating faster and harder and her breathing had shortened, as if she had run a great distance. "You are a strong man in heart and mind, and your legacy will not be diminished by those who are not worthy to speak your name." Saying the last words, she realized, much to her horror, that she had raised her voice and the authoritative tone made her cheeks heat up to the point she felt feverish. How could she have spoken so forcefully to this man? She had overstepped her bounds, and with head bowed, she offered her apologies.

"I have spoken out of turn, Your Grace," she murmured. "I cannot begin to apologize enough. Please, forgive me."

The Duke placed a hand on her arm. His touch was gentle and did not make her recoil as had that of Lord Clarkson.

"There is nothing for which to apologize," he said with a small smile. "You did as I asked and answered me as a friend would. For that, I am thankful. I will take your words into the greatest consideration." He glanced up to where the sun had last been. "Now, however, let us return to the house, for the sun has left us."

Jane nodded and then set out with the Duke by her side. Although it was dark, the white stones that made up the path guided their steps. And contrary to what the Duke said, she glanced over and saw light in his eyes.

***

The candlelight flickered, casting moving shadows on the wall as the steady patter of light rain pelted against the window. Jane sighed and then smiled as she looked at Samuel as he lay in bed, his eyes heavy. The young boy fighting sleep was inevitable, just as it was for other boys his age, for they wished only to keep a vigilance on the world around them.

"Miss Harcourt," he said, the drowsiness in his voice evident. "Do you have a mother?"

Jane stifled a sigh as she brushed back his hair. Memories of her mother came back to her and her heart constricted. "I did, but she has been gone for quite some time now."

His eyes searched her face. "Do you miss her?"

"Yes," she replied with all honesty. "I think about her every day. She was a good woman who was strong and had a kind heart." She smoothed out the blanket that covered the boy in an almost absentminded way.

"Father told me that my mother was a kind person, too. I wish I could remember her."

Jane's heart broke as she rose up from the bed. "I am sure she was, Samuel. Mothers tend to be kind and loving to their children, and some more than others. Now, it is time for you to sleep or you will be much too tired to go exploring and you do not want that, do you?"

"No, I have," -Yawn- "too much to do."

"Then I will see you in the morning."

The boy yawned again and his eyes closed. Within no time, his measured breathing told her he had fallen asleep. Taking the candle from the stand, she headed out of the room. Taking a final look at the boy, she pulled the door closed with a quiet click and almost screamed when she turned to find the Duke standing behind her. How was it he could sneak up on her at any moment?

"Your Grace," Jane gasped, her hand going to her breast.

"Forgive me for startling you, Miss Harcourt," he said. He glanced at the now closed door, a thoughtful look on his face. "I am fascinated by the way Samuel has taken to you, far faster than any other governess he has had before."

"Thank you, Your Grace," Jane said, the candlelight illuminating them both in the otherwise dark hallway. She knew not what else to say, so she remained quiet as the Duke looked down at her. He did not stand so close as to be inappropriate, but she found his nearness discomforting. Or was it exhilarating?

"You do not hesitate to look at me like you once did," he said. "I see your head held high."

Jane's heart skipped a beat. Had she offended the man? Her worry must have shown for the Duke smiled, his voice light and calming.

"I am glad to see it for no one should hang their head."

Jane breathed a sigh of relief. For the past week she had worried night and day about her outburst in the garden, and despite the fact that he had said she had done no wrong, she could not help but wonder if he would use her actions against her. A woman, especially a servant, did not raise her voice to a Duke no matter the reason.

"I have considered your words concerning my leaving the house and venturing into the town," he said. "I have decided to heed those words and do just that."

She could not stop the smile that spread across her face. "This is wonderful, Your Grace," she said in all honesty.

"This Saturday, I will take Samuel out in the carriage. Although I do not plan to go into the town proper, a ride beyond the lines of our property would do us both good."

Jane could not agree more and was pleased to hear his words. She could not imagine being tucked away for so many years, even if Wellesley Manor was a large and beautiful place in which to live.

"I know you will enjoy your outing," she said.

"*Our* outing."

"Pardon me?"

"I would like it very much if you would accompany us, Miss Harcourt."

Jane stared at the man. It was not the carriage ride through the country that stilled her tongue from an immediate response but rather the time spent with a man she to whom she could not help but feel some attraction. Granted, they would be in the company of young Samuel, but she could still not help but wonder whether spending too much time with the man was an unwise idea. She almost laughed at this. Here she was debating on whether she should be alone with a man and his son while she was standing alone with the man in a dark hallway.

"Excellent," he said before she realized she had agreed. She knew not if it was by magic or because of the smile on his face that had caused her to do so, but agreement she had made. "I will see you in the morning."

She watched as he walked away, his stride long and his posture impeccable. Soon, all she could make out was the light from his candle that allowed her to see only a silhouette of the upper part of his body.

Retiring to her room across the hallway, her thoughts were on the carriage ride as she changed into her nightdress. She smiled as she considered the conversations they could have.

However, when her eyes fell to the flame on the candle, she was reminded of the rumors. Then she laughed as she pushed aside the silly ideas that invaded her mind. She had to learn to trust the man who paid her wages, for he had yet to prove even a single rumor correct. She had never been a person to allow the words of others to decide the truth about another, and she was not going to start now.

As sleep overtook her, she wondered what the morning, and their short excursion, would bring, and if she should be afraid.

Chapter Eight

Jane slipped the white gloves over each hand. Although they were not yet ragged, the cloth had become well-worn and she would need to replace them soon. They were nothing like a woman of the *ton* would wear, but she was not such a woman, so they would be acceptable for this outing.

She gave herself one last look in the mirror and sighed. She had debated what she should wear and had finally chosen the blue dress again. Of course, she did not choose that particular dress to impress the man. It was her best dress and she would be in the company of a Duke. Was it not proper she wear her best dress in which to be seen while in the company a man of his standing? At least, that was her rationale.

After their carriage ride, Jane planned to visit her cousin. The thought of seeing Anne and the conversations they would have brought a smile to her face. She had so much she wished to share with Anne, but she also had to adhere to the promise she had made to the Duke; she would not share that which was personal to him.

As she made her way down the hall, she passed several servants, as well as the Duke's valet, Duncan. A clean-shaven, scrawny man who raised his nose in the air as if everyone besides the Duke was beneath him, the man made no indication he had even noticed her, but he did tend to be distracted most of the time. As a matter of fact, few looked her way, all preoccupied with their own duties to take notice of her passing. However, she did see the slight glances her way from time to time, but it was public knowledge that she would be accompanying the Duke and Samuel today. Their tongues would wag despite what she might tell them, so she ignored their surreptitious glances and instead decided to enjoy the day.

When she arrived at the front door, the Duke and Samuel were both waiting for her. They each wore a dark-blue coat and tan breeches with a white ruffled shirt, Samuel doing his best to imitate his father in every way. Although Jane had taken a brush to Samuel's hair, the dark waves had begun to curl once again on top of his head and now appeared as if he had not touched a comb or brush in weeks.

"Miss Harcourt," the Duke said with a bow. Jane could not help but notice the way his broad chest stretched the coat tight or how his breeches fit snuggly on his legs.

Samuel did his best to imitate his father, giving her a less confident bow than his father.

Jane took her skirts in hand and dropped into a deep curtsy. "Your Grace," she said before dropping into yet another curtsy. "Young Master."

Samuel made an attempt to stifle his giggles as Jenkins opened the door for the trio. The Duke gave her a smile and put his hand forth to allow her to be the first to pass through the front door. Outside sat a carriage adorned with the family crest on the door, much more elegant than the one that had taken her to Anne's to collect her belongings. Stained a deep brown, the carriage could have carried six people quite comfortably and had lush cushions with matching curtains that were drawn closed. This did not surprise Jane, for she knew this first step would be difficult enough for the Duke without the worry of someone seeing him. Well, at least he was making an attempt to leave his property, that was enough for the time being.

When the Duke took his seat across from her, she gave her a wide smile. Perhaps it was the excitement of leaving for a ride, or the thought of seeing Anne when they completed their excursion, but whatever the case, her cheeks burned and her breath caught in her throat. It certainly could not be the smile the Duke had for her.

The carriage lurched into motion and Samuel giggled in delight as he pulled back the curtain to look outside. It occurred to Jane that not only was this the Duke's first outing in many years, it was also Samuel's first. How sad that a boy his age was confined to the property and not allowed to explore beyond its lines. Granted, the lands on which sat Wellesley Manor were quite large, but to see so much more would be of great benefit to such a young boy.

"I do believe we could not have picked a better day for an outing," the duke said with a smile. Jane gave a polite nod. "The weather is perfect, and I believe the roads will give us no trouble despite the rain the past few days."

"I believe you are right, Your Grace," Jane replied with a glance out the window. "Notice how the birds are out, glad to enjoy it as much as we."

At the end of the drive, the carriage turned right onto the main road and the Duke took a sharp intake of breath. Although his posture was typically stiff, now it appeared to be rigid, unbendable. Samuel, however, only moved closer to the window and pressed his face to the glass to look out at the fields as they passed.

Jane had a desire to ease the Duke's mind, for his face was flushed and his hands grasped the handle on the inside of the door. "Are you enjoying the scenery, Your Grace?" Jane asked in an attempt to get him to look out the window and to ease his mind. However, his breathing had become hurried and the fear on his face worried her.

"Samuel, I believe that if you were to sit here, that would make it easier for you to look out either side you prefer," Jane said. Samuel readily agreed and wobbled when he stood to change places with her.

"Look at that tree!" Samuel shouted. "There is the biggest nest I have ever seen. Might we come and see what kind of bird lives there?" He gave Jane such an excited look she could only agree.

"Of course we will come," she replied. However, the majority of her attention was on the Duke. She had to do something to ease his anxiety, but she was unsure as to how. She knew it was not a fear of the movement of the carriage that had him gripping the handle so tightly his knuckles turned white. Even with the curtains drawn on their side of the carriage, she knew he struggled with the fact that someone might see his face. Perhaps going too far from his home during this first outing was a mistake. No man, however, let alone a man of title, would ever admit to such fear, and Jane knew that any words she would say to console him would only embarrass him more than aid him.

Yet, there was something she could do. With little movement, she eased her hand under the one which lay trembling at his side. At first, the hand was stiff and unyielding, but after a short time it began to close around hers.

When the Duke turned toward her, Jane felt her breath catch as he gave her a single nod. Although he spoke no words, he did not need to, for the grateful look he gave spoke volumes. The feel of his hand in hers sent a bolt of exhilaration through her and for the first time in many years, she felt a peace she had long forgotten. It was as if all the troubles of the world had abandoned her, and somehow the Duke of Fire had taken them all away.

Neither spoke a word as the carriage continued its trek down the road. From time to time, Samuel exclaimed about one thing or another but he took no notice of the hands clasped between them.

And although it was silly and unbecoming of her to do so, she imagined for a moment what life would be living with this man in a capacity more than a governess. Learning more about him and enjoying his touch and the security it provided. For though she had meant to provide him with a sense of confidence by offering her hand, in all reality it was she who had received the enjoyment.

Yet, dreams such as those were like the ones she had had as a child. There was never a chest of gold hidden away in the trunk of a tree waiting to be found, and she knew that dreams such as the love of a Duke for a woman such as she never did come true, for they were left to children to believe as much as silly women with unrealistic fantasies for their lives. Regardless, she held the hand and gave the man comfort, reveling in his nearness. Even though it would not last forever.

***

The carriage came to a stop, and Samuel bolted through the door and ran a short distance away, going straight to a large tree, his hand moving over the bark as if it held great fascination for him.

"Father," he said in an excited tone, "might I look around for a while?"

"Yes, you may," replied his father. "However, you must remain where

I am able to see you."

Promising he would, Samuel walked over to another tree, once again inspecting the rough bark.

Jane shook her head and laughed.

"And what do you find so humorous, Miss Harcourt?" the Duke asked, though is tone held amusement.

"Arthur, the son of the Earl, was the same," she replied as she watched Samuel flit from tree to tree like some small bird. "He always wished to explore or look for animals. I see now that all young boys seek adventure when they can."

"I must admit that it is true. When I was his age, I, too, took every opportunity to leave the confines of my house and explore my family's land." He let out a sigh. "I never knew I would one day find the same enjoyment doing it as an adult."

Jane nodded, understanding what he meant by the words. "I am happy that you came out today, Your Grace," she said. "I know Samuel is enjoying it and I presume you are, as well?"

The Duke said nothing for several moments, the only sounds the laughter of Samuel as he moved around the small expanse of woods. It was a beautiful spot where they had stopped with numerous trees that surrounded a large patch of deep green grass that the sun had yet to turn brown.

She wondered if she had spoken out of turn and was relieved when the Duke spoke.

"Although we are not far from my estate, I must admit it feels as though I am far away." He turned toward her. "Miss Harcourt, I speak no lies. I did consider your words all week, and they became a great encouragement to me."

Jane could not stop the smile that spread on her lips, and her heart went out to the man who stood before her.

"I wish there was a way to repay your kindness."

She laughed before she could catch herself. "Your Grace, there is no need. I am glad to see you out here. Knowing that our outing has brought you joy is more than enough payment for me."

The Duke smiled. "You truly are a wonderful woman. You have

brought a light to the life of both Samuel and me."

Without warning, Jane's heart soared. For a moment, she imagined the man putting his arms around her and pulling him against his broad chest to hold her close. If he moved to do so, she knew she would be unable to stop him. Not because he was stronger than she, but because she would not wish to stop him.

"I must admit that I feel the same. The fact that you have allowed me into your home has been a great honor, but to work with a child as bright and intelligent as Samuel is wonderful."

Several feet away, Samuel's voice came to them and they let out a small laugh. The boy was having a conversation with one of the trees.

"I have been thinking," the Duke said. "In the short time you have been with us, you have become more than just a servant. You have become an important part of our family, not only for Samuel but for myself, as well." He once again turned toward her, and she wondered if she would melt into the grass from the steadiness of his gaze. "I would like you to address me by my Christian name, which is Michael."

All breath left Jane's lungs. To be asked to do something so intimate made her unsure, but he was a Duke. Could she stop herself from doing his bidding? Would she want to?

"Thank you, Your...that is, Michael," she said. The use of his given name rolled off her tongue easier than she had expected, even though she had almost used his title instead. "I feel honored that you would allow me to do so." Her face was afire and she wondered if there was a stream nearby where she could simply jump in and cool herself before she smoldered to ash. Then it occurred to her that she had not returned the honor. How would her name sound from his lips? "If I am to use your Christian name, then perhaps you should use mine, as well."

The two stared at each other for several moments, neither speaking. The smells of nature wafted around them, and the sounds were muted in her ears. Although she had discounted any notion of romance in her life, for the first time, Jane began to wonder if love could be in store for her after all.

Chapter Nine

Michael watched as Jane stepped through the open gate and turned to close it behind her. She gave them a wave and then walked toward the small cottage at the end of the short drive. The woman's beauty was unmatched, her skin flawless, her gray eyes alluring. She had awoken desires Michael had long thought gone, not just with her looks, but also with her words. She had a kindness about her and her voice was soothing. Her smile brought a light into an otherwise dark world to which Michael thought himself accustomed.

As if she knew he was thinking of her, she turned one last time and smiled at him. He hid himself behind the curtain, of course, but she must have known he would be watching her walk away.

Earlier, fear like none he had ever known gripped him as the carriage made its way out the front gate of his estate. His worry was for the chance meeting of someone he knew, or even for someone he did not know. He could almost hear the whispers coming from their carriages, disgust at his face, curiosity for the beast within. And during that storm, the kindest gesture came to him as Jane placed her hand beneath his. At first, he refused to allow his weakness to show, for any woman who saw his fear would believe less of him. He also did not wish to give the woman any false ideas. However, he found himself allowing his hand to close around hers, and although there had been no contact by skin—her gloves kept that from happening—it did not matter, for the peace she transferred to him soothed his very soul. It was as if she held a secret about strength and generosity that she was willing to share with him.

His mind drifted further as the carriage made a turn to head back home. Standing beside the woman in the small clearing as Samuel played had relaxed Michael further. Somehow, with her by his side, he felt the madness that plagued him dissipate, leaving behind a calm he had not felt in many years. It was as if the man he had been before that fateful day so many years ago had returned, and despite the fact that more than likely he would return to hiding when the madman returned, he would enjoy it while it lasted.

Then he smiled. A lady such as she—she did not come from title or wealth, but she was a lady nonetheless—added a much-needed light in not only his life, but in the life of his son.

"I wish Miss Harcourt would return tonight," Samuel said with a sigh, breaking Michael from his thoughts.

"Is that so?"

Samuel nodded sadly. "She makes me happy," he said. Then he sat up straight and looked ahead. "And she is a good teacher."

Michael chuckled. "That she is," he replied.

The carriage turned onto the road that led to their house. Although he did not want to admit it to his son, he was going to miss Jane, as well, even if she was only away for one night. He let out a small laugh. He would fool no one but himself if he thought she was more than just a governess. The more he thought on how quickly they had grown close, the more surprised he was with himself. However, he knew in his heart it was right. He would have her join them for every meal, as if she were a part of the family, for that was how he saw her, a member of their family. To allow the woman to call him by his given name was ludicrous, but it felt right and moved in the direction he wished to take. No, in the direction he needed to take. He longed to love again, to have a wife and a mother for Samuel.

Yet, he knew that a woman as beautiful as she could never fall in love with a man who was as scarred as he. He was revolting to most but especially to himself. He knew in his heart that she was not a woman who could be bought or who would be influenced by title or position, for if she were, she would not have spurned the Earl's advances. Many women were set up with apartments by their employers when they became more than servants, and she could easily have used that to get what she wanted. However, she had left instead, without a reference and without severance. She had not told him any of this, but he had ways of learning these things.

No, Jane was one who would marry only for love, and he found himself jealous for the man who would win her heart.

"Your Grace," the driver said, startling Michael back to the present. The carriage had stopped in front of Wellesley Manor, and the door was already open. With a nod, Michael exited the carriage and was shocked to see his brother Robert waiting at the top of the steps.

"Robert. What brings you to my home today?" Michael said as he climbed the stairs.

Robert wore a sour look and grimaced at Samuel. "You should go to your room. Your father and I have some things to discuss."

Samuel gave his uncle a puzzled look and then turned to Michael, who gave him an encouraging nod. The boy bounded through the front door but glanced back before disappearing up the stairs.

Once the boy was gone, Robert turned back to Michael. "We had a meeting scheduled at two," he snapped. "I have other things I could be doing without wasting my time here waiting on you to return from who knows where."

Michael searched his brain for any memory of a meeting for today with Robert, or anyone else for that matter, and found none. "There was no meeting scheduled for today," he said. A feeling of frantic alarm poured over him, covering as thoroughly as any hot oil dumped over him from a murder hole could have. And it burned just as hot in his mind.

His brother took no note of his agitation, however. "I told you on my return from London that I would be here at two. Do you not remember?" It was then that he realized how he had spoken, for he reached out a hand and placed on Michael's shoulder. "Worry not, Brother. It is of no consequence."

"But it is," Michael whispered, the magic of the day now gone as the reality of his madness returned. When he looked into Robert's eyes, he saw the pain reflected, all caused by the malady Michael carried.

"No, it matters not. We are here now." He placed his hand on Michael's back to guide him through the door. "Where were you, if I might ask?

You have not left the house in five years, so I was surprised to learn you had gone out in the carriage. Was there something of such importance you had to leave?"

Michael sighed. His brother had always taken such great care of him. He was uncertain what he would do without his guidance and companionship. "Come to the study and I will explain there."

***

Robert paced back and forth in front of the empty fireplace. "I must admit I do not like you leaving the house, Michael. It is far too risky."

Michael had explained to his brother about his excursion and how much he had enjoyed it, but he had found his brother's reaction surprising.

"Miss Harcourt thought it was something I needed," Michael explained, "and I believe she was right."

His brother gave a short laugh and stopped his pacing to lean against the desk. "My brother, I have always spoken to you kindly and in truth, have I not?"

The words tore at Michael's heart. "Yes, and for that I am grateful."

Robert pushed himself away from the desk and gave Michael a stern look. "Then heed my words and listen carefully. Your memory is slipping, your forgetfulness has increased tenfold over the last few months." Michael nodded. What Robert said was true. He had been very forgetful as of late, and it worried him no end. "Then this woman, your new governess of all people, encourages you to leave. Why would she do that?"

Michael was filled with both anger and confusion at the tone his brother used with him. It was so unlike the man to speak to him like he was a child, and he was not about ready to allow him to begin to do so now. However, Robert gave him no chance to do so.

"She does not know the degree to which you suffer. Her actions, yes, they might have been out of kindness, as you have indicated, but she does not know the repercussions it would bring to you, or to Samuel."

Michael stared at the man. Repercussions of an outing? "Speak plainly, for your words confuse me."

Robert softened his tone. "What if you had had a lapse while away from the house? Do you believe that Miss Harcourt would have the skills to know how to handle such an incident? And what would that have done to Samuel? How would that have affected him?" He tapped a finger to his head. "Think, Michael. Do you wish to harm your son?"

"Of course not, but you do not honestly believe…"

Robert ignored his interruption. "What if you decide to leave again, this time with only Samuel, and you forget the boy? Or forget who you are? There will be no one there to help you, and I would want to kill anyone who tried to take advantage of your broken state. Not to mention the ridicule your son would be forced to face. You know that shame all too well, do you not? And the boy has enough to endure once he is at boarding school and his classmates learn who his father is."

Michael sighed. Everything Robert said was true and it broke her heart to think he could have endangered his son. The thought of the boy being left alone or perhaps something worse happening due to a bout of lost memory terrified him. "I understand." Fear gripped him and he fell rather than sat in a nearby chair.

Robert took the seat next to Michael. "There are times such as now when I worry I am going too far," he said. "It is just that I worry for you, and of course Samuel."

Michael stood and walked over to the window. Samuel was walking along the path, playing with two large rocks in his hand. His son, his only heir, was all that he had in this world, and the thought of ever forgetting the boy crushed him. Not only for the loss but what it would do to the boy himself.

"It seemed like a good idea at the time," Michael said in a low voice. His thoughts went to Jane and he wished she was beside him now. He needed her strength and the peace that seemed to radiate from her smile. When he turned back to his brother, the man had moved to the bookcase, a glass of brandy in his hand. Michael had not even heard him pour, which only concerned him more. Was he so unaware of what was happening around him that he did not hear even his brother pouring a glass of brandy?

"I have seen that look on your face before," Robert said in that quiet, calm voice on which Michael had grown to depend. "You have become smitten with that woman."

"That is nonsense," Michael said. "She is a governess and nothing more." However, was she nothing more? He was not certain.

He walked over to pour himself a measure of brandy. "I only had one love in my life, and she is gone. I have no time to win over another." The liquid burned as it traveled down his throat, but it was not an unpleasant feeling. Somehow it made him feel more alive.

"Elizabeth was a fine Duchess, a testament to the title she held," Robert said in almost reverence. "This woman, this Miss Harcourt, could never come close." Why did the man sound angry? "Mark my words, be careful of those who seek to be kind to you only because of your title and wealth, for that combination will drive anyone to look past your scars and guilt, and more so a governess. She will use you as much as anyone with ulterior motives to swindle you for their own gain."

Michael nodded. He had heard the stories about such people, women and men who had made their way into the good graces of a member of the nobility only to take what they could and run. People such as they were no better than a common thief.

Yet, could Jane be such a person? She had been so pleasant and understanding during their outing, but as he thought on it, he did find it odd how easily the woman looked past his scars when anyone else would have been horrified by them. He did not want to believe she sought after his wealth or his title, but there was no reason for her to look past his scars on his face. Nor the ones inside him for that matter.

No, Robert was right. Jane had to be watched closely, for if she did find a way to worm her way into his life, all she would have to do was wait for him to finally lose his mind. Then she would be able to rob him of everything he had and leave Samuel with nothing. He had to protect what was rightfully his, thus keeping safe what rightfully belonged to Samuel.

"Thank you, Brother. I will do as you suggest and do a better job of guarding myself. Now, let us discuss more pleasant things, like business."

His brother smiled as he followed Michael to the desk and took the chair across from him. If Michael could keep his mind on business, then perhaps he would not think on Jane. Unfortunately, it was not as easy as he had hoped.

Chapter Ten

The slow current of the brook flowed over the rocks at a steady pace as Jane dipped the stocking in the cool water. As luck would have it, the sun had moved behind a bank of clouds, providing Jane with some much-needed shade. Having changed from her dress into one of burlap belonging to Anne, Jane found the fabric much more irritating than she remembered.

As Jane scratched at her arm, Anne let out a small laugh. "You've been away not even two months and already you've grown soft. Is your skin much too delicate for normal clothing now? Or should I give you back your lovely silk dress so you can finish the washing in that?"

Jane caught the playful tone of her cousin's voice and laughed. "That is rubbish through and through," she said with a sniff. "It is the heat from the sun that is causing my skin to itch." She stood and placed the last of the washing in the basket.

"Well, aren't you quick to defend yourself," Anne said as she placed the basket on her hip. "Do you fancy yourself a Duchess now?"

"I am a governess and will never be anything more," Jane replied, though the sing-song in Anne's voice made Jane laugh again, and she gave her cousin a light push as they walked back to the house.

The two women headed to the line and Jane handed Anne a peg. She had shared some of her experience of her time at Wellesley Manor, but some she still kept to herself, just as she had promised she would.

"You still have told me little about the infamous Duke of Fire," Anne said with a casualness Jane knew as not true. "Or do you hold some sort of affection for the man?"

"There is little more to say about him," Jane replied as she attached a peg to one of David's shirts. "My requirements include young Samuel; I have very little reason to interact with the Duke."

Anne clicked her tongue. "Come now, cousin. Surely there is some tidbit you can share with me."

Jane shook her head. "I'm sorry, *cousin*, but there is nothing to tell."

Anne sighed. "Well, is there no handsome man to turn your head there? Maybe the Duke's brother? I hear he is quite handsome."

"Will you stop?" Jane said, doing her best to keep any heat from her words. "I have my responsibilities and that is where my energies are spent."

Anne stopped and turned to Jane. "Does that mean you have decided against finding love? Surely you want to marry one day."

Jane found herself biting at her lip. Although she still held reservation about the Duke, she had found his company quite enjoyable. Their outing earlier had brought about a peace inside her she had not felt in a long time. But love? Very unlikely.

"All right," Anne said as she threw a stocking back into the basket, "enough with the secrets. I've always known when you're keeping something from me, so who is he? The butler? No, men in that position are too stiff for you. Ah, I bet it's a stable hand. They're typically quite muscular and rather eye-catching." She leaned down and picked up the stocking once again and pinned it to the line. "One way or another, I will learn the truth and you know it."

Jane said nothing, unsure as to whether or not she should tell her about the outing she had taken with Michael. Granted, Samuel had been with them, but knowing Anne, the woman would have made a mountain out of a molehill.

Fortunately for her, she did not have to make a decision right then, for a rider appeared. The man dismounted, and though his clothes were well-made, she did not believe he was titled, although he did seem to have an arrogance about him as if he were.

"Oh, this should be interesting," Anne said in a whisper. "What has David done this time?"

The man walked toward them. He had a handsome face and his blond hair moving in the wind might have been appealing to most women.

However, something about him set Jane on edge.

"Hello, Bernard," Anne said as she picked up the now empty basket and rested it on her hip.

"Anne," he replied with a slight nod. Then he turned to Jane and bowed. "Good day to you, Miss. My name is Bernard Chandly. And you are?"

"Miss Jane Harcourt," she replied, unsure if she should curtsy. Anne certainly had not.

Bernard turned to Anne. "Has David returned yet?"

"No," Anne replied curtly. "He isn't due back until tomorrow. Is everything all right?"

He flicked a hand at her. "Oh, everything is fine," he said with a heavy sigh that said that everything was not fine. "Will you let him know that I am needing to speak to him at once upon his return? It is a matter of business."

"Of course," Anne said. "Good day to you, Bernard."

"Good day to you, Anne." Then he turned and bowed to Jane. "I hope our paths cross again, Miss Harcourt," he said. Then he took her hand in his and planted a wet kiss on her knuckles. It was difficult for Jane to not pull her hand away and wipe it on her skirts.

When the man was gone, Jane followed Anne back into the house. "What was that about?" she asked, her curiosity getting the better of her.

Anne snorted and shook her head. "Bernard fancies himself a businessman now. What those two are scheming about this time, I haven't a clue, but if David gets us into debt, I'll have his head."

"I take it they have had more than one scheme that did not go well?"

"You could say that. Bernard certainly was taken with you, though. I'm sure that dress had much to do with it."

Jane looked down and felt her cheeks burn. The dress was a size too small and emphasized her large bosom, showing more than she would have preferred, but Anne had always been smaller in stature and frame than she, so she was not surprised at the fit. It was not as if she thought anyone besides Anne would see her in it. Men tended to consider the outside of a woman to be much more important than what they had to offer on the inside, anyway.

81

"It matters not. I have no interest in the likes of him," Jane said in reply.

Anne said nothing as she gazed at her, and then she took Jane's hand in hers. "Follow me."

Jane allowed her cousin to lead her back to the brook.

"Sit," she commanded.

Jane did as she was told and sat beneath a large tree, watching the water's flow. What words of wisdom could the woman be ready to deal out to her this time?

"I don't understand you sometimes, Jane," Anne admonished.

Jane gave her a hurtful look. "Excuse me? What do you mean?"

"You have been blessed in this world," Anne explained. "You're educated, able to read and write better than most. Your beauty drives men mad with passion and women with jealousy. Yet you throw away every opportunity at love that is thrown your way. Why is that?"

Jane let out a sigh. Did Anne truly believe that someone like Bernard would be a good catch? "The places where I have found employment, the men…" she started to say, but Anne spoke over her.

"I know of these men; you've told me of them often enough. But you don't really believe that all men are like them, do you? Do you believe David is like them?"

"Of course not," Jane replied with a sigh. "David is a kind and gentle soul."

"Yet he cannot be the only one, can he? Surely there are more out in the world."

Jane nodded as her mind went to the Duke. He was kind and gentle, despite what she had heard about him. There was still the issue of the death of his wife, and yet Jane refused to be confronted with that.

Anne narrowed her eyes. "Someone has caught your eye and somehow that bothers you. Am I correct in saying so?"

Jane sighed. "Yes," she replied.

Anne took her hand. "You know you can tell me anything."

"I do, but there are some things that cannot be told."

"Trust me. I can keep your secrets; you know I can."

Jane worried her lip with her teeth. Should she share with this woman who she had trusted her entire life? Anne had never revealed any of her secrets before, why did she struggle now? She had promised Michael that she would not share about him, but she did not promise she would not share about herself. If he became a central part of her life, could she still keep that from her closest friend? Maybe she could share the truth about the man without revealing who he was.

"He is a very nice man," Jane said. "He is kind and gentle like David. But he also says things that I thought no man would ever say."

Anne gasped "What is that? He had best not have been indecent or he will be forced to deal with me!"

Jane laughed. "Of course not. How can a man be kind and gentle and yet be indecent at the same time? No, he comments about my spirit or my kindness. I believe he sees beyond this," she moved her hands to encompass her body. "We have connected beyond the outward, if that makes sense." She sighed. "I hope I do not sound mad."

Anne placed a hand on Jane's arm. "It makes a lot of sense. It's the first steps of a bond between two people, and it's a beautiful thing."

"And do those feelings lead to love, do you think?"

Anne gave her a sigh. "I believe they do. When David and I first met, there was that attraction many couples have—a physical attraction. We could not deny it. Then came the joy of seeing one another, the sharing of secrets and dreams. Yes, all these things may lead to love, but there are no guarantees."

"Nothing in life is guaranteed," Jane said as she thought about how she had found herself attracted to Michael when they first met, before she had seen his scarred face. However, she had told herself she could look past all that, and she realized today that it was true. She smiled as relief washed over her. Love? What a strange feeling it was. The poems never made it seem so strange.

"You make a very good point," Anne said. "Life gives no guarantees, but we do what we must to be happy."

Jane looked down at the brook and made a decision. "It is the Duke I speak of," she said in a low voice. What she had expected was to see Anne smile or perhaps ask a mound of questions. However, what she did not expect was the laughter. "And what is so humorous?" she demanded.

The laughter stopped and Anne took on a seriousness that appeared peculiar on the woman's face. "You mean…" She gaped at Jane, "the Duke of Fire?" Now she sounded astonished. "I thought you were making a joke! Jane, you cannot fall in love with that man!" She paused and took a quick glance around. "He's a murderer!" she whispered, as if saying so aloud would summon the Duke at that moment.

"He is rumored to be but has never been outrightly accused. Plus, I suspect that he is not. I feel this in my heart, as much as my thoughts. He is much too kind and gentle to have taken the life of anyone, let alone the woman he loved."

Anne tsked. "Jane, you are no longer the young naive girl you once were," she admonished as she pushed herself up from the ground. "Do you not see what he is doing?"

"He has done nothing."

"Ah, but he has. You said you feel something for him, did you not? Do you believe he returns your affections?"

"Perhaps," Jane responded with honesty. "I do not claim to love him; you were the first to use that word. What I do feel is a special friendship for a man who is hurting." Then it was her turn to look around, yet no one was there. "I am allowed to call him Michael. Surely that means something."

Anne sighed. "Yes, you are still very naive, even after what you have been through. Do you not see that he is using your goodness to lure you to his bed?"

"No. I do not believe it," Jane said, though she felt an uncertainty in her words. Could it be possible? Would he do such a thing? "He has made no attempt to touch me or press his lips to mine like the others have done. He is a kind man."

"Kind or not, he is a Duke, and you are a governess. Dukes simply do not become romantically involved with their governesses unless their only plan is to bed them." She placed a hand on Jane's cheek. "Even if he was not a murderer and is as kind as you say, a Duke would never marry the likes of someone like you. It's not possible."

A tear burned down Jane's cheek. "But today…the carriage ride. He talked of my words and how they helped ease his pain…" She felt no heat behind her words.

84

"Maybe they do help ease the guilt he feels. I don't know. However, Jane, you cannot have feelings for this man. He will only use you for his own needs, and once he's done with you, you will lose what little you have. But more importantly, he'll crush your heart. Let it go now before it's too late."

Jane stared off at the creeping brook and knew that her cousin spoke the truth. No man in his position would consider a governess for his wife. For his table, maybe. For his bed, definitely. But for his bride, never. The world simply did not work that way.

"I'm sorry to be so blunt," Anne said as she pulled Jane in for a hug.

"No, you are only telling me what I need to hear. I apologize if I became angry with you."

"There is no need to apologize," Anne said, releasing Jane from the embrace. "Do not be overly upset, for the right man will come along. One day you will look back and be happy that you did not waste your time— or your reputation—with the Duke of Fire. One day, the right man will come into your life, just you wait and see."

Jane nodded, although she struggled believing it as truth. What she feared at the moment, however, was that the right man had already come into her life and his title would always keep them apart, whether he wished to be with her or not.

Chapter Eleven

Samuel sat hunched over his desk, or rather a small table that acted as a desk—he had insisted on a piece of furniture to complete his work like his father—as he worked the set of sums Jane had assigned him. The end of his tongue flicked out as he worked, which Jane found endearing. However, Jane was not focused on the work the boy was meant to complete but rather on Michael, just as she had every day since returning from her cousin's house over a week prior.

Something had changed in Michael while she had visited Anne, for when she returned, she had expected to find the same kind man who had deposited her at the house of her cousin, for that man had laughed and smiled. Instead, the man who had taken his place upon her return was sullen and forlorn. Jane found she missed Michael's warming aura but she knew not how to approach him about this strange and sudden change. Although the avenue of communication had opened between them, and the Duke had said that she could speak freely, Anne's warning plagued her. Therefore, rather than confront him on his recent behavior, she remained silent. Although she saw him regularly, somehow they had returned to being strangers once again.

Not only had Michael's demeanor changed toward her, but he also no longer came by to check on the progress Samuel was making. No further invitations to dinner or to walk together in the garden were forthcoming. Jane wondered if she had somehow displeased the man. Perhaps her visit with her cousin had allowed him time to reconsider where she stood in the household, for there was no other explanation that came to mind. It was not that she wished to be higher than her station—she was no opportunist—however, she had enjoyed their interactions, whether they were short and to the point or long and meaningful, such as the day of their outing.

What surprised Jane the most was the loss she felt. Granted, they had only begun acquainting themselves with one another, but that day they had gone on their outing had been very special to her and she had thought Michael had felt the same. Their friendship, if one could call it that, had brought a warmness to her heart, and now it was gone.

"Miss Harcourt?"

Startled, Jane drew in a breath, her heart thumping. She turned to Samuel and smiled, hoping the boy had not noticed too much her distractedness.

"I am sorry, Samuel," she said, glad her voice told nothing of her momentary distress. "What is it?"

"I said that I've finished my sums." He picked up the paper on which he had been working, the ink smudged in several places as well as numbers that had been corrected with a large X over the original sum.

"Well done, Samuel," she said, glad to see that he had completed the work satisfactorily. "Your penmanship has improved exponentially since I first arrived. Tell me, how is it you do such a fine job at all of your studies?"

This seemed to tickle the boy, for he gave her a proud grin. "It can only be that I have a great teacher, that's why."

"That is very kind of you to say," Jane replied with a smile, "but I believe it is because you have applied yourself more since I have arrived. Never forget that you can become better at anything you wish—if you apply yourself. The more you practice at a task, the better you become."

"Yes, Miss Harcourt."

Jane rose from the chair and walked over to the window. Without turning, she said, "If you put away your things, we may go outside for a while. Would you like that?"

"Oh, yes, please!" Samuel said and Jane heard papers rustling behind her. She could not help but suppress a grin.

When she turned, however, she covered her mouth to hide her gasp, for in the doorway stood the Duke. He wore no smile, and Jane wondered if he was angry.

"Miss Harcourt, a word, please," he said, his voice returned to the formal tone he had used when she had first arrived. She was glad he had spoken her name first, for now she knew the invitation to use his Christian name was more than likely not acceptable.

Jane walked over and stopped to stand in front of him, and for the first time she saw the dark circles and redness of his eyes. "I am not feeling well and will retire to my room. Will you dine with Samuel this evening? I am afraid I am much too tired to do so myself, and I do not wish for him to eat alone."

"Of course, Your Grace," she said with a light curtsy.

"Thank you," he replied. "If any need arises, please send word with Duncan."

Jane nodded. She doubted relying on the valet would be of much help if something terrible happened, he did very little even for a man of his high position, but at least the man could carry messages.

After Michael had gone, Jane turned to find Samuel standing behind her, a worried look on his face. "Is Father not well?" he asked.

Jane brought herself down so she could face him. "He is just fine," she said. "He only wishes to lie down and rest for a bit. However, I do have some wonderful news."

Samuel's eyes widened. "You do?"

"Yes. I will be your guest for dinner this evening."

He appeared very pleased by this and said, "Will you wear the blue dress again? Please?"

This made Jane laugh. "I suppose I can," she replied. "Do you like it?"

The boy shrugged. "I think it's pretty, and…well, Father said you look beautiful in it."

Jane's breath caught in her throat. She doubted very highly that the man had said such a thing. However, if he did not say it, then what had compelled the boy to say he had?

"Sometimes Father talks aloud when he thinks no one hears," Samuel said as if reading her mind. "I heard him say it after you had dinner with us."

Jane rose and tapped Samuel on the tip of his nose. "That was kind of him to say so," she said. "However, you do realize that sharing what someone says of another person when that someone had no intention of telling said person is a form of gossip?"

Samuel gasped. "I didn't know," he said, clearly finding the idea unsettling.

"Well, now that you know, you must remember that such idle talk is something we should not do, for it is the root of most rumors, and few enjoy rumors, especially when they are about themselves. Now, we should be on our way if we are to have time outside before we ready ourselves for dinner."

As she followed the boy down the hallway, Jane could not help but smile thinking of the Duke and that he found her beautiful in her blue dress.

***

Samuel and Jane had enjoyed their dinner together making polite conversation throughout the entire meal. Samuel seemed delighted to play the host, but he had refused to take his father's place at the table, insisting that "only my father has a right to that chair. That is, until I become Duke". Jane was glad he was still too young to realize that the only way he could assume his father's place was when his father died.

Now, Jane sat in her usual place on the edge of his bed as she waited for him to close his eyes and fall asleep. She was unsure why this had become a regular occurrence, but she found she took pleasure in their bedtime routine of reading together several pages from their current story, followed by Jane pulling the blankets up to Samuel's chin. Then she would sit with him until his breathing became even. Perhaps she indulged him all too much in this, but she would not have it any other way.

When she had been in the employ of Lord Clarkson, Lady Clarkson had insisted that staying with Arthur was simply a way to mollycoddle the boy and had forbidden Jane from entering his room once he had been put to bed. Unfortunately, this meant that if the poor boy woke from a nightmare, he was well aware that no one would come to his side to comfort him regardless of how afraid he became. Arthur, being the clever boy he was, however, had found a way around this rule: if he found himself troubled by bad dreams, rather than cry out and await the arrival of someone who could console him, he instead ran to Jane's room. Jane never told the boy's parents for by him going to her room, she was not disobeying the Countess's rule. Not once did she return to Arthur's room once he went to bed.

This night, Samuel lay heavy-lidded as he stared up at the canopy above his bed. His face was scrunched tight, as if he was deep in thought.

"Of what are you thinking?" Jane asked as she placed a hand on the blanket that covered his chest.

He shifted his gaze to her, his face remaining pensive. "Is my father your friend, Miss Harcourt?" he asked in the innocent manner of children.

She raised her eyebrows at him and then looked toward the window. Rain tapped against the glass as broad streaks of lightning flashed in the sky. She collected her thoughts before responding, wishing to answer as carefully as possible. "Your father is my employer, and I work for him. So, I would say that our relationship is one based on a business arrangement."

He sighed as if the weight of the world was on his shoulders. "Do you not like him?"

"Why, yes, I like him. He is a very kind man and smart, just like you."

He pursed his lips and tilted his head at her. "Well, I like you a lot."

She stifled a giggle. "I appreciate that," she replied. "And I like you a lot, too."

"I wish you were my mother."

Jane thought her heart had dropped to her feet as tears welled up in her eyes. "That is a very kind thing to say and it makes me happy. Thank you."

"Then you'll become my mother?" he asked hopefully.

She brushed back his hair as she fought back the tears. The boy did need a mother in his life, though sadly, it would never be her. "It is not my choice to make. One day your father will meet a woman and they will fall in love and marry. Then she will become your mother and love you as much as your father does."

Samuel went quiet for a moment. "Is it my reading?" he asked. "I can work harder on improving it. Then you will be happy to be my mother."

Jane could no longer hold back the tears and she brushed them aside as she leaned over to kiss his forehead. "You must understand that it is not because I do not think you worthy to be my son, nor have you done anything to upset me. You see..." she wondered how to explain the concept of love between the sexes when she, as an adult, struggled at times, "a man and a woman fall in love and then get married. Your father, though a very kind man, is not in love with me. Do you understand?"

He sighed. "I think so." He took on an auspicious look. "But maybe one day he will be."

Jane stood and gazed down at the boy. "One day he will meet a woman and fall in love again, but for now, you must focus on your studies...and getting to sleep."

"All right, Miss Harcourt, I will."

She picked up the candle from the bedside table and smiled down at him. "Good night, Samuel."

Before she got to the door, he said, "Miss Harcourt?"

She stopped and turned around. "Yes, Samuel?"

"Father loves you, you know. Why else would he say you look beautiful in your dress?"

Jane gave him a smile and shook her head. "Good night, Samuel," she said before closing the door behind her.

When she arrived at her room, she changed into her nightdress and walked over to the window. She found the patter of the rain calming as she thought on Samuel's words. Why, indeed, did his father say he thought her beautiful in her dress? If he had said such words. Yet, he had commented on her eyes and how she brought light into his life. Men such as he did not speak such words lightly.

Anne had said that men in the Duke's position oftentimes found ways to lure women to their bed; however, Jane found herself doubting those words. The man held many secrets, and although Jane wished he would share them with her, she feared he never would. Or perhaps she feared what those secrets could be. But no, she still did not believe him capable of killing his wife, so any secret he was willing to share she would accept and then somehow help the man heal.

Slipping beneath the covers, Jane put out the candle and closed her eyes. She cared for Samuel, and his words about needing a mother pulled at her heart. However, the boy was young and did not understand the intricate web love wove. And although the thought of being wed to the Duke made her smile, she knew dreaming about such notions was foolish and a waste of time. She had a commitment to instructing Samuel; anything beyond that was beyond her control.

Chapter Twelve

*J*ane found herself in a field of rich green unlike any she had ever seen before. A light breeze caused her hair to flow behind her and her skirts to rustle. Beside her stood the Duke of Fire, his hand firmly gripping hers as if he meant to never let it go. No one knew the kind and gentle heart this great man had, nor would anyone be able to know the bond he shared with her. It was beautiful and, one would say, magical. Yes, that was what brought these two together—magic, a power and a feeling that could not be described in any other way.

"Miss Harcourt," Samuel said as he ran up to them, his happy smile lighting up his face as it always did when they took these excursions.

Jane laughed. She was his mother now, and she found it amusing that he would still refer to her by her old title.

His hands came to her shoulders and he gently shook her.

"Miss Harcourt."

Jane opened her eyes and found her heart racing as Samuel gently nudged her again. Although there was no candlelight, she did not need it to hear the fear in his voice.

"Miss Harcourt, Father is in trouble," he said, a frantic ring to in his tone.

She sat up in bed, her mind trying to comprehend what the boy was saying. "Samuel, what is wrong?" she asked. The only light came from what remained of the fire in the hearth, but she could make out the boy's features well enough, and the frantic look he gave her made her jump from the bed.

She lit a candle and followed Samuel down the hallway, or rather the boy pulled her. Thunder drowned their footsteps in intermittent blasts, and Samuel squeezed her hand in fear with each loud rumble.

The Duke's voice carried to her ears before they reached the door to his bedroom, and she stopped to listen.

"The fire! Elizabeth! The fire!" he was shouting.

Jane glanced down at Samuel, who wore a look of stark terror, his lower lip quivering.

"It is all right," she said to the boy with as much calm as she could muster. "He is having a nightmare, nothing more."

Samuel gave her a dubious look, and then the Duke cried out again. "Put out the fire!" The anguish in the man's voice was enough to have Jane doing what she never would have imagined she would have done in normal circumstances. She entered his room.

Once inside, her jaw fell open, for the Duke did not appear to be asleep but rather was sitting up in his bed, his face panic-stricken.

"Father?" Samuel called out as tears streaked down his cheeks.

"There is a fire!" the Duke yelled. "You must leave!"

Samuel began to wail. "Father!" Then he turned to Jane and gave her a beseeching look. "Please! Help him!"

"Samuel, I need you to do me a favor." When the boy nodded in agreement, she continued. "You must return to your room at once. Do not worry; I will help your father, and when I have calmed him, I will come to see you. Can you do that for me?"

Through his tears, Samuel nodded again and then turned and left the room, stopping long enough for one last look before rushing down the hallway.

Once she was certain Samuel was gone, she hurried to the bed and realized that the Duke was no longer yelling. Instead he was staring out her, a glazed look in his eyes. She went to speak, but his hand shot out. His grip was firm and heat radiated from his skin.

"Elizabeth, I am sorry," he said in a loud whisper. "I am so sorry."

She managed to remove his hand from his arm, with some resistance on his part, and then helped him lie back down in the bed. She reached out and placed a hand on his forehead and was shocked to find that he was burning up with fever.

"Michael," she said when he tried to sit up again. "I need you to lie back down." She pushed him gently back into the pillows and he did little to resist her.

"The fire. She is still inside."

Jane's mind spun as she considered what to do. It was much too late to call for a doctor. Plus, he would do little more than what she could do on her own. The first thing she needed to do was to lower his fever.

She hurried to where she knew the maids kept rags they used for cleaning and grabbed several. When she returned to the Duke's room, she was pleased to find the pitcher was full of water, so she poured some into the bowl and carried it to the bedside table. Dipping one of the cloths into the water, she wrung it out and placed it on his forehead. His first reaction was to shy away from what had to feel like freezing water in his fevered state, but soon he allowed her to use another cloth to dab at his cheeks.

"The fire," he moaned.

Jane was glad he was no longer shouting. "The fire is out, Michael," she whispered as she wiped at his brow. "You are safe now, everyone is safe."

Her words seemed to calm him and he settled into a restless sleep.

For several hours, Jane replaced the heated cloth from Michael's forehead with a cooled one. From time to time, he would open his eyes and speak.

"Elizabeth, you came back to me," he said at one point.

"All is forgiven," Jane whispered back. "But you must rest. We will talk later of this."

Then he would close his eyes once again and sink back into the pillows.

At one point, she realized that his sheets and pillow cases were soaked with his sweat, so she returned to the linen closet, took out new linens, and return to replace clean for dirty. It was not an easy task, but she had seen it done before. All she had to do was roll him over on one side, remove the wet sheet on that side and replace it with a clean one. Then she would roll him back over onto the clean sheet, remove the wet from the other side and pull the clean sheet tight. The task done, she returned to replacing the cloths.

"Do you forgive me?" he asked, though his eyes remained closed.

"Yes, Michael," she whispered. "I forgive you."

This time he seemed to accept her words, for he fell into a deep sleep. That is until he began to toss and turn once again. This time she unbuttoned his dressing gown and placed a cold cloth on his chest. The dressing gown was also now soaked, so she removed it. She had no idea where to find a clean gown, and he still had a significant fever, so she simply pulled the covers up over his unclothed torso.

Then began the fight with the covers. At one point, his body would shake so violently that she thought she would be thrown from the bed, and she would cover him with a second blanket. Then later, he would kick the covers off, complaining that he was much too hot. Time and again, the battle raged between him kicking off the blankets and him shivering and needing them replaced. However much she had to fight him, she continued with her careful ministrations, until, finally, he slept once again.

The light haze that came just before the rise of the sun crept into the room, waking Jane from a light sleep. She stretched and yawned, the small bones in her back cracking as she did so. When she glanced down at her patient, her breath caught in her throat—there was no rise and fall of his chest under the blankets.

"Michael?" she whispered, fearing the worst. When he did not respond, panic washed over her and she pulled the covers back and placed a hand on his chest. She breathed a sigh of relief when she felt his heart beating within him, and she slowly moved the covers back up to his chin.

"Do not leave me," he croaked, his hand trembling as he grabbed her wrist.

She easily removed his hand and placed it beneath the covers. "I will never leave you," she said. "Never." The thought of one day leaving this man, and Samuel, of course, made her chest constrict, and she wished the words could be true. However, she knew that, eventually, she must leave, for once Samuel was old enough to attend school, she would have fulfilled her responsibility of caring for him and would no longer be of use in the Blackstone home.

"Good," Michael mumbled. "For I care for Jane and I believe she cares for me."

Jane bit at her lip but knew the words the man said were the result of a fever and did not come from his heart.

"When she enters a room," he continued, "it is as if the light I need enters with her. She makes me happy, Elizabeth; I hope you understand that."

Tears fell as Jane reached up and brushed his hair from his brow. "Then I am glad you are happy," she whispered.

A peel of thunder sounded in the distance; whether the remains of the night's storm or the beginnings of a new one, she did not know.

"I do not know if I make her happy," he mumbled, his face twisted in concern.

"You make her very happy," Jane told him as she replaced the warm cloth for a cool one.

He said nothing more, and she returned the cloths to the basin. She had not yet spoken to Samuel, and the boy had to be sick with worry. When she arrived at his room, he was indeed awake, though his eyes were so heavy, it was a struggle for him to keep them open.

"Your father is better already," she assured the boy. "He just needs to rest now from his nightmare."

Samuel gave her a weak smile. "Thank you, Miss Harcourt," he said before closing his eyes and immediately falling asleep.

Jane pulled the covers up to the boy's chin and kissed his forehead. "Bless you," she whispered, glad he was now at ease.

When she returned to the Duke's room, she found him mumbling words she was unable to hear. Leaning over, she put her ear close to his lips.

"Don't leave me," he said quietly.

Smiling, she took his large hand in hers and watched his shallow breathing, glad to see the movement under the covers once again. Whether the bond between them was that of only friendship, or of love, she did not know, but as the rain once again beat on the window panes, she knew that for at least this night, she would, in fact, not leave the man's side.

Chapter Thirteen

*T*hick smoke filled his lungs as Michael held his young son to his chest. Covering the boy, he hurried through flames that singed his clothing, his hair, and even his skin. The boy screamed, but Michael was unsure if it was due to fear, pain, or the heat. He suspected it was all three.

Michael's eyes watered and he squinted through the haze until he found an exit. His legs wobbled beneath him, threatening to give out, but he had his son to consider. So, with a roar, he pushed forward, using the last of his strength to break through the door and out into the cool night air. It was a stark contrast to the flames behind him, and the shock made him shiver. He collapsed to his knees as Jenkins rushed over and took Samuel from Michael's arms while Michael coughed and gasped in an attempt to force fresh air into his smoke-filled lungs.

Something shifted behind him and Michael pulled himself back up. He had to get back inside; Elizabeth was still there. However, before he could move even a foot forward, he heard a scream just as the roof tumbled down.

Michael's body shook, his eyes flying open, and he realized he was back in his room, whispering apologies to Elizabeth. His heart soared when she whispered back, letting him know that all was forgiven.

Then he told her about Jane, for he could not allow himself to love another until Elizabeth allowed him to. That was what she did. In the coolness of her touch, she gave him permission to love another. That was his Elizabeth, always giving, always understanding. It was strange that a man who had become known as the Duke of Fire, a man who was believed to have killed his own wife, was so afraid of being alone. However, as his fear grew once again, it came to a halt when a small hand took his and held it, providing him the peace he so desperately needed. Thus, with that peace flowing through him, he slept.

Sometime later, he did not how long, his eyes flickered a few times, though he was still too weak to open them. His mind began to bring up images and feelings of the night before. He had felt the fever come over him, had felt his body ignite. And then? Then someone was whispering to him and caring for him.

He smiled. That person had been Jane. Yes, the governess had come to his side, comforting him and letting him know that all would be well.

Managing to open his eyes, his heart skipped a beat as he looked down at his bare chest. The very woman who had brought him comfort lay with a hand on his chest and her head cradled in the crook of her arm, her breathing slow and rhythmic. She still held his hand—it had not been a dream after all!—and he reveled in the closeness. She had kept her word and apparently had fallen asleep while watching over him.

Jane wore only her nightdress and he allowed his eyes to soak in all of her beauty, from her well-sculpted face to the contour of her sides. A longing burned within him, a longing to kiss the woman and hold her against him. He wanted to run his hands along her curves, to touch her soft skin. Yet, she was not his to be so intimate.

Carefully, he moved her hand and began to pull away from her. A small smile played on her lips, but she did not wake. Once he was free of her, his foot found the floor and he made an attempt to pull himself up. On wobbly legs, he stared down at Jane, and his mind was taken back to the last few weeks. He had kept his distance from her in an attempt to block not only his mind, but also his heart, to keep himself from falling in love with her. However, he now knew that those attempts had been futile. She had captured his attention in so many ways, and trying to deny it would not make those feelings go away.

He made his way around the bed, holding on to the posts to steady himself. When he reached Jane, he leaned over and moved her hair from her face.

"You are so beautiful, Jane," he whispered, "and yet, you do not see it. But I do."

For a short time he watched as she slept, until the first rays of weak light flooded into the room. The servants would already be starting their daily chores, and although most never ventured this far into the manor, he needed to wake her before Dalton came in. It certainly would not do to have his son's governess found sleeping at his bedside, even if she had been his nurse for the night.

He was worried he would be much too weak to carry her from the room, but he would try nonetheless. She barely moved as he attempted to pull her into his arms. It took several attempts, but finally, he picked her up—she weighed very little—and made his way, stumbling, from the room.

Jane shifted and pressed her face to his chest. "I care for you, Michael," she mumbled.

He shuddered lightly at her breath lightly moving the hairs on his chest. Perhaps he should have donned a shirt before attempting to move a half-clothed governess from his room. The thought of someone catching him in such a predicament made him chuckle, and he had to stop and lean against the wall halfway down the hallway before he could continue his trek to her room.

When he finally had her safely tucked under her blankets, he gazed down at her beauty. Surely no creature under the sun was lovelier than she. Leaning over, he wished to kiss her plump lips, but instead he placed a gentle kiss on her forehead and then quietly left the room. He would allow her to sleep; Samuel's lessons could easily be completed another day.

Heading back to his room, he began to prepare for the day ahead. Despite his exhaustion, he had too much work to complete to be abed. Plus, whatever had occurred during the night was now gone, and he would not allow it to get the better of him.

***

Michael walked down the garden path, Samuel at his side. At the end of the path was a gate, and he stood looking out over the large open field, his mind looking within at images of he and Elizabeth enjoying an afternoon riding horses and taking long walks together. Although Wellesley Manor had been their country home and not their main residence, they spent their first summer here enjoying the open air and the fresh, green grass. How he missed those days with her.

He closed his eyes and pictured her hair coming loose and flying behind her in the light breeze. He could almost hear the echoes of her laughter and the smell of her soap as they danced together in the wide-open expanse.

The gate creaked and Michael opened his eyes. Samuel had already run through and made his way toward the top of a nearby hill, so low it could barely be called a hill at all. Though the grass was still damp from the previous night's rain, the hot sun was now out soaking up most of the moisture.

"Your Grace!"

Michael turned to see Jane hurry toward him, her skirts caught up in her hands so she would not trip over them. She stopped beside him, puffing breathlessly, her eyes red and the skin around her eyes puffy. It was clear she was still exhausted missing so much sleep the night before.

She put her hand on her side as if it ached her. "I apologize! I cannot believe I slept to such a late hour. Past one!" She clicked her tongue in annoyance. "Samuel has missed his morning lessons already, and for that I am sorry."

Samuel came running back to them. "Miss Harcourt, do you want to see me roll down the hill?"

Michael ruffled the boy's hair. "Go on ahead, Samuel. We will meet you there."

The boy whooped and took off at a fast pace, not once looking back to see if they followed.

Once Samuel was out of earshot, Michael turned back to Jane, her gray eyes pulling him in as if they had some sort of magical ability. "Jane," he said quietly, "I have told you before to call me Michael, have I not?"

She gave him a quizzical look, but it only lasted a moment. "You did," she replied, yet her words held a bit of skepticism.

"As to your tardiness, your rest was well-deserved. Thank you for last night; your words and…well, your words were comforting."

Her cheeks turned a delectable shade of pink. Surely she remembered falling asleep in such an intimate position, or at least she realized that he had carried her back to her room.

"I am glad to see you feeling better," she said. "However, I would advise you not to exert yourself too much today. In all honesty, you should be abed resting."

He chuckled. "I suppose I should be, but I prefer to be out while the weather holds. Come, join me." He offered his arm and she placed her hand on it without much hesitation. Then together they made their way up the small slope. Samuel laughed as he ran through the grass, he arms open wide so they skimmed the seedy tops of the grass stems.

When Michael sneaked a quick glance, he saw that Jane still suffered from a reddened face, and he kept back the questions he had been wishing to ask her concerning the previous night. Whatever had happened, he did not wish to embarrass her further. However, the need for him to tell her how much he cared for her burned inside him.

"Jane, I must ask something, if I may be so bold," he finally said.

She gave him a simple nod just as they came upon a felled tree in a small clearing. Samuel was there with a stick, poking at the mud and muttering to himself words Michael could not hear.

Michael decided to continue with his questions. "Most women your age have already found a man willing to marry them, or are actively searching for such a man. Why is it that you do not? Surely you have had lines of men vying for your attention." She said nothing for a moment and he realized how forward his question sounded. "I was much too bold," he said, looking at the ground. "Forgive me. It is not my concern."

She turned toward him, her hands wringing in front of her. "Your question is not out of line; it is one my cousin Anne has asked me time and time again." A smile played on her lips. "A few men have sought after me, but most of those men were already married, so you can imagine that I could not accept any suggestions of a relationship with them."

Michael chuckled. "No, I suppose you could not at that. But what of those who were yet unwed? Surely you could have married one of them."

She sighed. "For a long time I did not believe I was beautiful enough to catch the eye of a man, though many men have told me differently. My eyes, as I have told you before, give me a sense of shame, so in that shame, I do not meet their eyes. Few men find such meekness appealing, or so I have been told. However, you have helped me with my confidence, and though I still do not see myself as lovely, I do not see myself as horrid as I once believed."

Michael gave her a smile. In just a few weeks, she had gone from a meek and humble girl to a woman with confidence, and he was glad for that. "It is good that you see yourself as others do," he said as he plucked a blade of grass from the ground and twisted it in his fingers.

Her cheeks turned a deep crimson. "No man has ever asked me about my dreams or has seen beyond what lies on the outside. This bothers me, for one day, I will grow old and gray, and then what? The beauty of a person eventually abandons us all, and then what becomes of that person? In all reality, beauty lies within, does it not?"

Michael nodded but said nothing.

"So few men see women in that light, and I used to believe none could. Now, however, I can see that, with you, I was wrong." She smiled and bit her lip as if she had more to say, but she remained quiet.

Michael studied her face and soaked in her lovely features. He wished he could kiss those plump lips, embrace her tightly, and show her how much he cared about her.

However, before he could speak the words on his heart, Samuel came running up. "I found a crawler!" he shouted. "He is horrid looking!"

Jane laughed and Michael turned toward his son. There was much to think about when considering Jane, but right now, his focus must be on his son.

***

Later that evening, Michael sat in the library before a dying fire, his thoughts on the changes that had come over him since the previous night. Granted, it was much too early to see whether or not he had been remade; however, there was a lightness to his soul that had been missing before. The burning fires that had plagued his mind seemed to have been extinguished, replaced by a soft glow, something much more soothing. It was a wonderful feeling, and he wished for it remain for always, and he knew Jane was at the foundation of that change. Yet, would she stay with him to see that this return of the man he had once been would be the man who remained?

As it was, that choice was not up to him. No, the decision was Jane's. Her earlier admittance of caring for him had left him in a state of wonder and had chased off the horrors that plagued his sleep. That peace had even remained after napping in the afternoon. That in itself was miraculous, for he never had a reprieve from the terrors of that night when his wife had perished in the fire.

The question remained as to whether Jane's caring was for a friend or was it more than that? Michael found himself wanting to ask, but he worried that, if he were to inquire and she only desired his friendship— which he would accept in a heartbeat—, would his question make her uncomfortable, and then subsequently causing her to leave?

He let out a sigh and took the last swig of his brandy. Setting the now empty glass on the table, he rose to make his way to bed. Then the light of the moon caught his attention and, rather than retiring, he walked out onto the veranda and made his way down the moonlit path.

The air was crisp but not overly cold, yet after sitting next to the fire, he still felt a shiver. Or perhaps the trembling came from his confusion over Jane. He knew that even if Jane did not care for him as he did her, she had given him strength. She had done what he had been unable to do; that is, to walk into the fire of his life and guide him out to safety. For that he would be forever in her debt.

Looking up at the stars, he thought of his time with Samuel today and how reclusive they had become. The time had come to put the rumors of the Duke of Fire to rest, not only to allow the Duke of Hayfield to emerge, but to pave a safe path for his son to take over the title. Samuel would not have to carry the burden of what his father had done, not if Michael had anything to do with it. Jane was right. If the *ton* wished to speak ill of him, let them do so to his face. Now was the time to regain his rightful place in society, and hopefully it would be done with Jane at his side.

It was at that moment that he wondered if the woman truly could read his thoughts, for the sound of someone walking down the path behind him made him turn and smile, and Jane came to stand beside him.

Chapter Fourteen

Jane had watched Michael from her window as he moved down the path under the light of the moon. Her heart beat against her chest as she thought of the previous night and more particularly this morning. She had woken briefly and found herself cradled in his strong arms, feeling safe against his broad chest as he carried her to his room. In the back of her fatigued mind, she knew he should not be up and about carrying a governess through the vacant hallways after the night he had endured, but she was much too tired to protest.

She had not meant to fall asleep beside him, had even promised herself she would not do so, but he was so comforted when she held his hand that she could not get herself to release it. Whenever she did, his undecipherable mutterings would return, and she feared he would relapse into his fevered state once more.

A sigh escaped her lips as she thought about the things he had whispered, the words she had been able to understand. The guilt he felt over the death of his wife was so great, easily determined by his need to apologize for whatever wrong he had done. Jane, however, felt no remorse for forgiving the man on behalf of his wife, for she could not allow him to carry that burden any longer. It was a wonder the man had not been ill before last night, although perhaps he had been and she had not been told.

Then her mind turned to his confession of his fondness for Jane. Yet, did Michael truly care for her? A governess was barely a step above the housekeeper, so why should she believe that a Duke had any level of affection for her? Most people, her cousin included, would laugh at such a notion, but Jane found herself in a conundrum. She needed to know what he had meant by his words, even if it meant being ridiculed by the man and she leaving in the wake of his laughter.

Jane stiffened her back and smoothed out her skirts. Now was as good a time as any to make her inquiries. At what other time would she find herself alone with the man where no one else would be able to hear?

She made her way down the stairs and out onto the veranda. She could just make out Michael halfway down the path, and her heart leapt to her throat. What was she doing? What if he rejected her? Not only would she surely lose her position at Wellesley Manor, but the thought of leaving Samuel alone bothered her greatly. Not seeing Michael, however, would devastate her.

That was the word that fit the situation perfectly—devastate. To have your whole world and what you cared for taken away from you. It had happened when her mother died, and she feared it would be the same if Michael sent her away for her foolishness. Yet, she needed to know, so she gathered her courage and moved down the path.

Coming to stand beside him, she gazed out toward the horizon, just as he did, enjoying the numerous stars that lit up the sky. She considered for a moment that it would take a hundred years to count them all, but there was no need for that. Their simple glow provided more than enough enjoyment without knowing their numbers.

"Over the last few months I have done a lot of thinking," Michael said, breaking the silence of the night. "In all that time, I have realized how precious life is. For years, I have resided at this estate, fearful of what lay outside it. Though I blame it on the *ton* and their dreadful rumors, I now realize that it has been more than that."

Jane's heart told her that the man was struggling to find words to express his feelings, so she reached and took his hand in hers. The act had calmed him before, perhaps it would do so again.

He glanced down at her, his eyes glinting with unshed tears. "You must understand that, until last night, I have lain blame on myself for what transpired the night of Elizabeth's death. And now I realize…" He shook his head and looked back up at the sky, "the fault is not mine. I tried to save her, but I could not. Now, I believe—no, I *know*—she understands that, as well.

"The rumors that have been spoken about me," he continued, "say that I burned down my own estate in order to kill my wife. How such horrible gossip is allowed to flourish is beyond me, but I have no control over what others say about me. However, I wish to tell you what happened, for you are the only person I care about and whose opinion of me matters."

He turned and gazed down at Jane, and she said nothing, allowing him the decision as to when he would begin his tale, for she understood that it would be difficult for him to share.

"I had left London earlier than planned and wished to surprise Elizabeth by returning home early, so I had my driver push hard through the night. I saw the fire raging in my home from the main road." He cleared his throat. "There was chaos all about as servants came rushing from the home. However, above all their shouts I could hear Samuel crying, drowning out all other sounds that came to my ear. So, I ran in, the fire burning my clothes, my hair, but I was able to reach him and take him out to safety.

Jane felt a hot tear roll down her cheek. She could not imagine the horror of that night, and her heart broke as he continued his story.

"However, Elizabeth was still inside. I handed Samuel over to Jenkins and went back for her, but you see, the fire was too great, its heat burning me. The pain was greater than I could take." He brought his hand up to the scars on his face, and the pain and grief of the man's tale shattered Jane's heart. She thought he would be unable to go on, and yet he continued.

"Alas, I had to retreat or die myself, and I never found her before the roof caved in, crushing her beneath the flames and debris."

The quiet clenched the air around them as Jane wiped at her eyes, understanding now the torment the man felt. The guilt of not being able to save the woman he loved.

"You did everything you could," she assured him. "No one could ask for more, nor could one expect anyone to be so brave as to enter a burning house to rescue someone, especially someone so well loved."

Michael nodded. "I understand that now, but for so long I thought I had lacked the courage to continue on through the flames, to burn even more of my body if it meant saving Elizabeth. It is why the guilt and shame have driven me to madness, or near to it, and has kept me from traveling beyond the boundaries of my property." He sighed. "Now, however, I feel more at peace and will take the advice of someone dear to me." He smiled down at her. "I will no longer be known as the Duke of Fire, a man who withers away as the seasons change. For I am Michael Blackstone, Fourth Duke of Hayfield, and I will no longer live in fear."

His declaration brought great joy to Jane and she found herself wrapping her arms around him and pulling him close. She knew she was being all too forward, but nothing could have stopped her from doing so, nothing at all, especially when his arms closed around her, as well. She laid her head against his chest and listened to his heartbeat.

"I am so happy for you," she said when the embrace broke. "I am happy you have moved on from the guilt that was not yours to carry. Thank you for sharing your story, and your heart, with me. This trust you have for me will never be violated, this I promise you."

"I know," he said in a soft voice. "From the moment I first saw you, I knew that you could be trusted. I cannot explain it, but it is true. I plan on leaving my estate more often and reintroducing myself to society. What I wonder is…would you be at my side when I do so?"

Jane could have leapt into the sky from this request, for her fears were now tempered. She had not misread his intentions. "I would love nothing more," she whispered in response. Then, summing all of her courage, she spoke again. "I want you to know, I have great affection for you."

"As do I for you," he said. Then he lowered his head and their lips pressed together in a kiss that left Jane melting in his arms. Electricity coursed through her limbs and congregated in her stomach, a strange, but wonderful, feeling that she never wished to lose. For a brief moment, her mind recalled what Anne had told her, to be careful not to be wooed by his words. However, she pushed those thoughts away, for she was not being pulled in by words, but rather by her heart.

When the kiss broke, she felt a loss, and she had to grab onto his arms to regain her balance.

"How are you able to care for me when my face looks as it does?" Michael asked.

She rested her hand on his scars and caressed them lovingly. "They are a testament to your strength and character, and like the rest of you, they bring me joy."

They stood staring at each other for several more moments and then Michael started back toward the house, his arm holding hers. "Now, how should I make my reintroduction into society?" he asked. "I imagine that simply walking through the village will not be enough."

Jane laughed. "I think you should host a grand ball and invite everyone. Let them see the new Duke of Hayfield in his new home, and allow them to marvel not only how handsome he is, but also how strong he is."

Michael joined in her laughter. "That is a wonderful idea," he said. "I will have the invitations printed at once. It will be the grandest of parties. And you could…" His words trailed off and he turned to her, worry on his face.

She already knew what worried him, and resting her hand on his chest, she smiled up at him. "There are many things you will need to do for yourself," she said. "I will continue to do my work with Samuel, for that is my duty. Whereas yours is not to have to explain why your governess is at your side during the most important night of your life. Slay only one dragon at a time."

"You do understand?" He shook his head. "How could I think you would not?"

She smiled at him once more before they returned to their journey back to the house. Her arm was still in his and she marveled at the feel of being so close to him. It was the most wonderful feeling in the world, much like the feeling that was within her heart.

***

A cool breeze made the branches on the trees dance as birds sang and the sun shone down on the gardens. To Jane, the world was perfect. It had been three days since Michael kissed her, and since then, Jane had never felt more alive. It was as if the air around her had the remnants of a lightning strike, and Samuel's laugh or the smile that played across

Michael's lips only added to the wondrous feeling she had—the most wonderful feeling Jane had ever experienced in her life—and she suspected that it would only grow in time.

Much of her life had become fantastical. How was it that she, a governess, had found someone who had the ability to make her life have more meaning? How could a Duke see a woman in her position in such a way? A Duke from whom others kept their distance?

Yet, when she thought on the past few months, she smiled. Indeed, she did know how it happened. She had been willing to look past that which could be seen and search for what dwelt inside. What she found was the kind soul of Michael, and she had had the confidence that, one day, that kindness would emerge for others to see. And it did. However, it was not only the change in him that brought about this sense of euphoria; she was changed within herself, as well. Now she saw herself as others did, a woman of beauty, and the torments of the other children no longer echoed in her mind. Her eyes, which she had thought for so long were a curse, now served as a blessing and were greatly admired by the man she for whom held a great affection.

Before taking on the position of governess, she did not know love, at least not the kind of love a woman has for a man. However, she suspected that what she felt for Michael was quickly becoming what she imagined it would be like. The thought both scared and excited her greatly, for if you give your heart to someone, there is a chance for hurt at some later point. Yet, although it was a great risk, it was one she was willing to take.

"I have never seen Samuel so taken to reading," Michael said, breaking Jane from her thoughts.

"He has come to love it as his ability has improved," Jane said as she watched Samuel, who sat beneath a tree, a book in his lap, appearing engrossed in the story.

"For which I am indebted to you," Michael said with a smile. "I fear that I may never be able to repay you for the changes that have taken place inside these walls."

Jane smiled and shook her head. "There is nothing for which to repay. The changes we have all experienced came from the heart; therefore, no debt exists and no payment is ever needed."

Michael chuckled. "I suppose you are right once again," he said with a wink that caused her cheeks to burn. "By the way, I plan to take Samuel into town this Friday and would like for you to join us."

Jane felt a sense of pride that Michael was taking such a grand step. "But of course," she gave in a ready reply. "It would be my pleasure."

"There is a dressmaker that creates the finest dresses outside of London, and I would be honored if you would select a few for yourself. I would pay for them, of course, if you allow me to do so."

Jane turned to him. "I cannot accept such a gift," she said with a gasp. "I will be able to afford my own soon, and…"

"You must accept, for to refuse my kindness would bring me great sorrow." He gave her a fanciful bow that made her giggle.

"Very well, then. I accept." Her eyes lingered on how handsome he was in his dark coat and breeches. When she realized he knew she was staring, however, she quickly cleared her throat and turned back to watch Samuel, who remained reading beneath the tree, his nose still in the book. Although the idea of spending the entirety of every waking moment with Michael, she knew she had work to do.

"Samuel," she called out, "why not put away your book and we will play a game of Cat and Mouse?"

Michael laughed when the boy groaned. "Most definitely change has come to Wellesley Manor in so many ways."

"And when it is time to stop playing and return to his reading, he will moan then, as well," Jane said with a laugh as she allowed Michael to help her rise from the bench. "Thank you," she said, her face on fire.

"Such is the life of a boy," Michael said.

"So I am led to understand," Jane said with a laugh. "Would you like to join us?"

"Alas, I must return to my work. However, I forgot to tell you that my brother and his wife will be joining me for dinner this evening. I would appreciate it very much if you would join us as my guest. I wish to share the good news of me rejoining the world again and what better way to do so than to have you there with me?"

Jane found herself caught up in the man's eyes, and she could not think of anything better than to spend an evening with him. "I would be honored," she said with a light curtsy, which only made him laugh. She gave him a wide smile and then went to join Samuel in the open field.

When she turned back, Michael was already gone, but she had little time to consider him, for Samuel was quick in the chase. However, in that sliver of time, she wondered about the encounter she had with Michael's brother, Lord Robert Blackstone. Lord Blackstone was a great worrier when it came to his brother, so perhaps seeing that Michael no longer wished to be confined to the house would make the man happy.

Happy. Yes, that is certainly what Michael made her.

"Got you!" Samuel said as he touched Jane's arm and scurried off to wait for her to chase after him.

Chapter Fifteen

For reasons she could not identify, Jane had never felt so nervous in all her life. Not only would she be dining with the Duke once again, but Lord Blackstone and his wife would be joining them, as well. Where she could be herself with Michael now that they had professed their feelings for one another, she was unsure whether she should attempt to act the lady of nobility in the presence of people with whom she had very little acquaintance or was there some other manner in which she should conduct herself. To make matters worse, this would be her first encounter with Lady Catherine Blackstone, and the idea of spending the evening with a woman of the *ton* had Jane's stomach in knots.

Jane closed her eyes and took a deep breath. It was not as if she was some sort of country bumpkin; she had some of the best training available to one of her station. She had nothing of which to be ashamed, so she squared her shoulders and took one last look in the mirror. Her hair was perfect with its flowing curls and flowers mixed in, and her dress was more than adequate—a green muslin with white lace, certainly not her best, but nowhere near her worst. She also had a posture that could rival any royal court. Yes, she was ready.

As she made her way down the stairs, she heard the murmur of voices in the drawing room. Had Lord and Lady Blackstone arrived early? Jane had hoped to be waiting for them when they called, but now she would be the one all eyes were on when she entered the room. Her head spun for a quick moment, but she pulled herself to together and walked through the door.

Michael and Lord Blackstone rose as soon as she entered, and Samuel gave her a wide smile.

"Miss Harcourt," Michael said as he walked over and gave her his arm. "You have already met my brother Robert."

"Yes," Jane replied with a curtsy. "My Lord."

"It is good to see you again, Miss Harcourt," Lord Blackstone said before taking her hand and kissing her knuckles.

"And this is Catherine, Robert's wife. Catherine, this is Miss Harcourt, Samuel's governess."

The woman could only be considered a great beauty with her striking blond hair and clear blue eyes. "Miss Harcourt." She rose from her chair and looked Jane up and down approvingly. "My husband mentioned that Michael had a new governess but he failed to mention how lovely she was."

Jane gave her a shy smile. "Thank you for saying so."

"Well, shall we head into dinner?" Michael asked.

Before he could offer Jane his arm, Lady Blackstone took Jane's hand and pulled her close. "We women must stick together, should we not?" she said as she led Jane to the dining room.

"I suppose we should," Jane replied, although she felt more than a bit disorientated.

"As I was saying," Lord Blackstone said as they took their seats at the dining table, "I still firmly believe that women have no place in business. Their ability to rationalize is not at a level with that of a man, and thus they simply cannot be as successful in such an arena. It would be like sending in the secretary to fight the gladiator." He laughed heartily at his own joke, and his wife raised an eyebrow at Jane, who had to stifle a giggle. The man was arrogance incarnate, although it did not surprise her in the least. She remembered her brief encounter with him soon after she had arrived and had not thought much of him then. At the time, she was uncertain what about him bothered her, but after his opinions thus far, it was clear that she had not been wrong in her assessment of the man.

"That may be so," Michael said as he took a drink of his wine. "However, as instructors, especially for children, they do quite well. Samuel has improved greatly in his studies and now I oftentimes find him with a book in his hand whereas before getting him to do any amount of reading was as difficult as pulling a carriage mired in the mud."

Samuel grinned at the praise from his father.

Robert, however, did not seem impressed. "It is because the boy is a Blackstone," he said with a snort. "We are gifted in many areas, and it is only natural that he has taken to his education."

Jane gripped her fork a tad tighter. She was not looking for praise from the man, but it was clear he would never be one to give her even the slightest acknowledgment for her contribution to Samuel's education. The boy was bright, there was no doubt, but he had not learned what he knew on his own. Then she loosened her grip. The opinion of such a man had no bearing on her abilities. Plus, it was only how Michael viewed her that mattered.

"Now, what I would like to know," Lord Blackstone said through a bit of food, "is why you have decided to invite your servant to dine with us."

Everything around Jane began to spin. The man's words reminded her of the warning Anne had given her—that someone such as herself was not, and could not be, like these people. Unfortunately, Jane had begun to believe the fantasy, and what Michael's brother said brought her back to reality as easily as a jump into an icy pond.

"Miss Harcourt is not a servant," Samuel said angrily. "She's a governess."

"Samuel!" Michael admonished. "That is enough."

The boy lowered his head. "I'm sorry."

Michael gave the boy a single nod and then turned his attention back to his brother. "I am grateful for the contributions that Miss Harcourt has made to this household," he said as he shot her a smile. "It is because of her wisdom that I have decided to host a ball."

Lady Blackstone gasped, and Lord Blackstone set his fork down on his plate with a clatter. "A ball? What ball?"

"The one I will be hosting here at Wellesley Manor," Michael replied, unperturbed by his brother's reaction. "I will be reintroducing myself to society. No longer will I hide behind these walls in shame."

The room went eerily quiet, and the air seemed to cool considerably. What she had expected was his brother to smile, or at least offer up words of encouragement. However, what the man said came as a shock.

"Surely you do not mean to do this. There are dire consequences to such rash actions, and with your current...forgetfulness," he glanced at Samuel who did not appear to be listening, "I believe you would be making a grave mistake."

Michael let out a heavy sigh and signaled a footman to remove their plates. "I do mean to do as I say, although I had hoped to have your support."

"I believe it is a wonderful idea," Lady Blackstone said in a quiet voice.

Lord Blackstone turned and glared at his wife. "The men are talking. Please, do not interrupt."

The woman nodded and looked back down at the table. Jane was furious; to see a woman treated in such a disrespectful manner was horrible and demeaning. However, she also knew that no matter what she said, her words would only make matters worse, so she remained quiet.

"Let us retire to the library and discuss this further," Michael said.

Jane turned to Samuel. "I believe it is time for you to go to bed."

Samuel nodded, pushed the chair back from the table, and silently walked out of the room.

Jane smiled at Michael. "I'll see to him," she said and she followed behind the boy. In all honesty, she was glad to be free from the animosity of the room. However, she did worry that Lord Blackstone would talk Michael of out hosting the ball, and Jane knew that doing so would only send the man spiraling out of control. Yet, she was just the governess; what did she know?

***

After putting Samuel to bed, Jane sighed and stretched. The boy was much more tired than she had suspected, which explained his short outburst during dinner. Although she was appreciative of his attempt to defend her honor, Jane knew that the boy speaking out as he did was nothing short of rude. She was never a firm believer in children being silent unless spoken to, but she did realize that they lacked the skills and knowledge to input their opinions at such a young age, at least at such a gathering.

She tugged the door closed behind her, careful not to be too loud, when a hand shot out and grabbed her arm. She spun around, ready to scream, and was surprised to see Lord Blackstone standing there.

"Lord Blackstone," she said with a sigh of relief. "You startled me."

The man glared down at her, the glint in his eye frightening her. "What is the meaning of your game?" he asked as he pushed her against the wall.

Jane winced at the ache in the back of her head where it had hit the wall behind her. "I-I'm sorry, My Lord," she stammered. "I have no idea what you mean."

"Do not play innocent with me," he said through gritted teeth. "I told you my brother is unwell and should not be leaving the house. Now I find that you ignored me and have encouraged him to do exactly that."

Pain shot through her arm, which he still held as he pressed it against her body. "My Lord! You are hurting me!" she said, though it was difficult to breathe, not only from the pressure he was putting on her body, but the fear that gripped her.

"I see now," he said in a low, yet harsh, voice. "You think you're not a woman of lower means. Do you believe yourself to be one of us?" Jane shook her head, but he snorted. "Do not lie to me, girl. I see the way you look at my brother, and I do not like it. You are nothing but a servant, despite what my nephew says, and I will not stand by and watch as you seek to take his fortune. You will never be a Duchess; do you understand me? Never!"

"I seek no such thing from him," she gasped, hot tears filling her eyes. Not from fear now, but from anger. How dare he accuse her of such nonsense! Regardless, she would not give this man the benefit of seeing her cry. "I have no interest in title or wealth. I only wish to see him get better, and leaving the house is a good place to begin."

"You are a liar!" he seethed.

"Robert?" a woman's voice said from down the hall. "What is going on?"

Robert stepped back and Jane sighed with relief. "Nothing. Miss Harcourt and I are simply having a conversation."

"Well, your brother is waiting for your return," she said simply.

"I am on my way," he said, not taking his eyes off Jane. Then he leaned in and lowered his voice. "Heed my words. You will never get another position as governess if I have anything to do with it." And with that, he walked away.

"You look as if you have seen a ghost," Lady Blackstone said as she walked up to Jane. "Are you all right?"

Jane wished to reply that no, she was not all right and that the woman's husband had just accosted her, but she could not get the words to come out.

"Come with me," Lady Blackstone said. "We will have something to drink in the drawing room. I know I certainly could use it after this evening."

With a nod, Jane replied, "Yes, that would be nice."

The two women walked down the hall and made their way to the drawing room. As Jane followed the blond beauty, she wondered how such a kind woman could have married such an angry man.

Entering the drawing room, Lady Blackstone went over and poured them each a glass of brandy. "Men are an interesting sort," she said as she handed a glass to Jane. "They seem to believe that, the angrier they become, the more important their words are." She laughed at this.

"I suppose that is true," Jane said, although she did not see Michael in that category. Yet, she was not about to admit to this woman that she thought so specifically about her husband.

"My Robert is like that," the woman said with a sigh. "I suspect his words are far from kind. Would you not agree?"

Should she tell this poor woman about how her husband had treated her with such disdain in the hallway before her arrival? However, what would that accomplish? It was obvious that the man treated his wife no better. "I am sure your husband his many good qualities," Jane lied. "He is firm in his beliefs, is all, My Lady."

Lady Blackstone gave a short laugh. "We really must dispose of these formalities," she said, "at least when we are alone. Please, call me Catherine." She placed a hand on Jane's arm. "And do not fear telling me the truth. I will not be angry."

Jane let out a small sigh. Perhaps sharing what had happened before the woman's arrival would be all right after all. "Lord Blackstone was angry with me for encouraging His Grace to leave the house, although I still do not understand why. Surely he would like to see him brother improve?"

Catherine rose and returned to the liquor cart. "I was afraid he would do something like this," she said with a sigh. She poured another glass of brandy. "Would you like another?"

Jane looked down at her untouched glass. "No, thank you."

The woman shrugged and replaced the stopper. "You see, when Robert loses his temper, he becomes a tyrant. But I can assure you, he truly is a gentleman."

Jane hid her doubt by taking a sip of her brandy. "I am sure he is."

"Well, let me be the one to apologize for his behavior toward you and seek your forgiveness."

"Yes, of course," Jane said, shocked that a woman of her standing would be find a need to do such a thing for a governess.

"Thank you, my dear," she said as she retook her seat. "You must understand that Robert has good reason to not wish Michael to leave the house." She swirled the amber liquid in her glass as she paused. "I'm not sure where to begin, but I guess the night of the fire is as good a place as any."

Jane sat up, curious to hear what this woman had to say.

"You see, after the fire and the loss of Elizabeth, Michael had so much guilt that it has driven him to a certain…madness, if you will."

Jane leaned forward. "I do know of his episodes, but I can assure you he has moved past that. The guilt he once carried he has now dealt with and moved on from it."

"May I take a guess at something?" Catherin asked. Before Jane could reply, she continued. "I imagine that Michael has told you that his guilt plagues him and that somehow you have offered him kind words that have suddenly freed him of that guilt. Am I correct in saying this?"

"I have helped him, but I believe he came to that conclusion on his own."

Catherine sighed, as if she carried a heavy burden. "Jane…may I call you Jane?"

"Of course."

"Well, Jane, you are a beautiful woman, and I can see that you have a strong, but kind, countenance. However, facts are facts. As a governess, you are a servant in this house, no matter what Samuel might believe."

"I do not try to give myself airs," Jane said.

"No, I suppose you do not. Yet, Michael has taken a liking to you. I have seen the way he looks at you. And you him."

Jane bowed her head. What this woman said was true, but surely it was not unheard of.

"I saw the same look on his face with the last governess." Catherine's voice was soft, but she might have slapped Jane on the cheek with what she revealed.

"You do not mean…?"

Catherine placed a finger on Jane's chin and forced her to look at her. "It is how I knew it was your words that led him to release his guilt, for I had heard the same from Miss Hester in this very room."

"This cannot be," Jane said, her voice choking. "He is a kind man."

"Yes," Catherine said with a sigh. "I would be the first to defend his name against anyone who spoke against it. However, he led Miss Hester to his bed and then when he tired of her, he threw her out onto the streets." She gave Jane's hand a gentle squeeze. "It is why my husband used such harsh words with you, for he does not want another woman to lose her virtue because of Michael's madness."

Jane searched the woman's face for any sign of a lie, but her tears of confusion blinded her. "It cannot be true." She looked back down at the glass of brandy, finding it difficult to comprehend what she heard.

"It is. And to Michael wishing to return to society or to host this ball? Robert worries that his brother will become the sinister man he was before the fire."

Jane's head shot up. "I do not understand. What do you mean 'before the fire'?"

Catherine shook her head. "Oh, he has been with many women. It was why he was away from Elizabeth that night; he was off visiting one of the hussies he kept on the side. It is what drives his guilt. You see, Robert's concerns are more than justified. Michael is slowly losing his memory, and Robert does not want the family name ruined for Samuel's sake."

Jane nodded slowly, finally comprehending the wisdom and worry of the woman before her. "I will do what I can to watch the Duke, if you would like," she said, her voice faint.

"That will be helpful," came Catherine's reply. "However, it is important that you continue on as normal so Michael does not know that you are helping Robert. If he were to find out you have betrayed him, I am unsure how he will handle it. The most important thing is that you must guard your heart, for Michael has a way with words and I would be greatly troubled if you were hurt in all this."

"Thank you," Jane responded. Could it be true that Michael was trying to woo her just to get her into his bed? However, had she not already encountered such a man in her last position? Perhaps her current employer used different tactics to lure his servants, but the result would be the same.

Her heart and mind warred with one another, but one thing Jane knew, she had to be careful from this moment forward. She would be vigilant and then ask Michael questions when the time was right.

Chapter Sixteen

Two days had passed since Robert and Catherine and come to dine with him, yet Michael was still troubled by his brother's words as they drank alone that evening.

"I am telling you, Michael," Robert had insisted, "that woman is after your wealth."

Michael shook his head. "No, I do not believe it. She has done nothing to make me believe that. Not once has she asked me for anything."

"Mark my words, she is up to no good. I guarantee it."

By the time his brother had left, Michael began to have doubts, but he still was not completely convinced that what his brother said was true. What he saw was a woman with an unselfish manner who had the best interests of Samuel and himself at heart, and he could never imagine her deceiving him in such a way. However, the seed had been planted and Michael struggled to shake off the idea, as awful as it seemed.

"Your coat, Your Grace," Dalton said, breaking Michael from his thoughts as he walked toward the door.

Michael stopped and sighed, allowing the valet to help him don the coat. Then he stopped. "What is this?" he demanded. "I specifically requested the blue coat, did I not?" The man was getting older, but that did not give him the excuse to ignore his master's requests.

"Your Grace," Dalton said in his simpering voice, "You told me…" He stopped and looked down at the floor. "My apologies, Your Grace. I will get your blue coat at once."

As he turned to leave, Michael caught his arm. "What did I tell you?"

"It does not matter, Your Grace. I'm afraid in my old age, I must have misheard you. The fault lies with me."

122

"It does matter. What did I tell you?" he repeated with more force.

"Your Grace requested that his black coat be prepared for today and to have the blue mended," the man said with great reluctance.

Michael gave him a nod. So, it was happening again; his mind was worsening though his heart had never felt more alive. Here he was sure that the madness would dissipate with his newfound freedom from the guilt he had carried; however, this incident was only a reminder that one day he would forget everything.

"This coat will do," Michael said with a sigh as he stretched his arm once again to allow the valet to put it on him.

As the man helped prepare him for the day, Michael realized that he had been fighting his brother's advice because he was afraid of the truth: he was truly losing his mind. As Dalton brushed out the coat, Michael's mind went to Samuel and he feared what would happen to the boy as Michael descended further into madness. Thankfully, his brother and Catherine would look after the boy, raising him to be the man he was meant to be. The thought saddened him, but he was not one to turn away from the truth.

"Shall I mend your blue coat, then, Your Grace?"

"Yes, thank you," Michael replied, though he did not remember what exactly needed mending.

The man nodded his head and left the room.

Michael walked over to the large mirror and gazed at his reflection. In just an hour's time, he would be leaving with Samuel and Jane to go into town, something Robert had been adamantly against. Now doubt made him question that decision. If he could not remember something as simple as the color of the coat he had asked his valet to ready for him, how could he take such a large step as to go into town? What if he endangered his son in the process as Robert had suggested?

Glancing over to the dresser, he went and opened the top drawer and removed a chain of fine silver that held a pendant of blue sapphires. It was a present he had given Elizabeth during their first year of marriage, and as luck would have it, she had kept it here rather than at their home, which meant it had not been lost in the fire.

"She is after your wealth." His brother's words played in his mind and

made him cringe. Although the idea of doing so twisted his stomach, he needed to test the woman to assure himself that what he believed of her was true. Such fine jewels would attract any woman's attention, but most especially one filled with greed.

Clutching the necklace in his hand, he left the room and waited for Jane to come down the stairs.

"I apologize for being late," she said with a wide smile. "I had forgotten my gloves and had to return to retrieve them."

"They look beautiful," he said and was delighted to see her cheeks redden.

She wore the blue silk dress she was fond of wearing, and later he hoped she would select another of the same color as one of her choices for a new dress.

"Blue suits you," he said, "and with your eyes, I thought these might complement them." He held up the necklace and waited to see her response.

"What a lovely piece," she gasped. "The blue in the gems are the brightest I have ever seen." Then she laughed. "Not that I have seen many sapphires in my life, of course."

"Well, they were Elizabeth's, and though it may seem crass, I thought they would suit someone such as you." His heart raced as he moved toward her. "I would very much like for you to have them."

Her smile widened and his heart began to sink. So, Robert had been right after all. Not only was she after his wealth, but she also found no issue with taking something that once belonged to his former wife.

"Although your offer is kind," Jane said, her hand closing around the pendant as the chain swung down, "I could never accept such a gift. For one, it belonged to your wife and should be given to Samuel first so he can give it to a woman of his choosing." She placed the necklace in his hand and wrapped his fingers around it. "Second, even if that were not the case, I do not need expensive jewelry to make me feel beautiful. You do that for me."

Michael's heart leapt as he realized what a fool he was to believe what Robert had told him. His heart had not deceived him; she truly had a kind spirit and was a woman who held no amount of selfishness.

Slipping the necklace into his coat pocket, he looked into her soft gray eyes. "I understand your concern, and I thank you for your honesty." He offered her his arm. "Are you ready for our outing?"

"I am quite ready. However," a look of concern crossed her face, "are you certain you are ready?"

To have a woman worry for him as she did made his soul jump for joy. "It has been some years, but I am ready to make my first appearance," he said, the nervousness he had been feeling melting away with the touch of her hand. "And with you joining me out there in that big, wide world, I will have the strength I need."

Jane stood on the tips of her toes and gave him a quick peck on the cheek. "Your strength is your own, Michael," she assured him. "Never forget that. Now, I believe Samuel has been ready for practically hours to take this journey into town, so we should probably be on our way."

Michael could only stare at her. The woman was all the strength he needed. It was the strength he would need for the time ahead. For the first time, he began to consider that there was a chance he could ask to be his wife.

***

"Father, why is Miss Harcourt leaving us?" Samuel asked as the woman entered the dress shop.

Placing his hand on the boy's shoulder, they began to walk. "Miss Harcourt is going to purchase some new dresses, and it would not be fitting for gentlemen such as we to be seen in such a place. But do not worry, she will be joining us again later."

The boy gave a nod, although his face still showed reluctance at leaving the woman behind. Perhaps he was concerned she would not return, which was ludicrous, but there was nothing Michael to do to ease the boy's mind.

Michael had instructed Jane to purchase as many dresses as she saw fit. Yet, he had a feeling she would only choose two, for she was not greedy, and he would have to chastise her later for it. Playfully, of course.

As they passed another shop, a man looked at Michael and then turned again to stare. Then he hurried his steps as if he had suddenly remembered that he was late for an important meeting.

Yes, the Duke of Fire is out. Run as fast you are able, Michael thought, yet he wore a smile despite the fact he should have been angry by the man's reaction. Michael had confronted his greatest obstacle—himself—and he now walked with confidence. Although Jane denied it, it was the strength which came from the memory of her words that helped him as he took each step.

"Your Grace!" Alan Shafer, a graying man who owned the local butcher shop, called from his shop door as he gave Michael a deep bow. "It has been too long."

Michael stopped and smiled at the man. He was one of the many shop owners who had always been kind to Michael, as well as Elizabeth, and it was clear the butcher had not forgotten him.

"It has been far too long, Shafer, but I am no longer going to be a stranger."

"Very good, Your Grace," the man replied. "And who might this young gentleman at your side be?"

"This is my son Samuel. Samuel this is Mr. Shafer. He owns this butcher shop."

Mr. Shafer squatted down to eye-level with the boy. "It is a pleasure to meet a fine gentleman such as yourself, my young lord."

"Thank you, sir," Samuel said. "I enjoy being a gentleman." His voice held such a sincerity that Mr. Shafer chuckled, as did Michael.

"We best be on our way," Michael said, "but I will have an order coming to you soon for a ball I am hosting."

"Very well, Your Grace. I will make sure only the finest cuts are delivered."

Michael nodded and walked away. His first conversation had gone much better than he had expected, and he could not wait for more. Granted, it had been with a man of the working class, but regardless, he still saw it as a success. Then a couple approached him, both of them wearing familiar faces from long ago. They had once claimed his friendship, but as the rumors spread concerning the death of his wife, their invitations had stopped. Although it had caused him sorrow before, it no longer did so.

"Your Grace," Lord Percy Hughes, the third Earl of Bramblestoke, said, his eyes wide. Lady Mary Hughes stood gaping at Michael, looking as if she had seen a ghost, but quickly recovered and dropped a curtsy before him. "It is an honor, Your Grace."

"Hello, Hughes. It has been a long time, has it not? I feel as though we have not spoken…in years."

The man straightened and jutted out his chin. "It is true, Your Grace. I hope I have caused no offense by not dropping by to call on you after the death of your wife, but we wanted to give you time to grieve. Is that not true, Mary?" The woman beside him nodded, although all she seemed capable of doing was to stare.

"Well, I have grieved long enough," Michael said.

"That is wonderful news, Your Grace," Lord Hughes said. "And may I say, it is wonderful seeing you again."

Michael smiled as his hand went to Samuel's shoulder. "I knew you would be happy, and that is why I look forward to seeing you both at my ball, which will take place in a month's time. The invitations will be sent out shortly, but I thought you should be the first to know."

Lord Hugh's face went an off-white. "Of course, Your Grace." He swallowed visibly. "What an honor."

Michael suppressed his smile. He knew that Lord Hughes was worried about how it would be perceived that he was told of the ball in person, and he knew the man's wife to be an incredible gossip. He wanted everyone to see that their idle rumors were unfounded and that he was now happy once again. He also knew, however, that Lord Hughes might need some sort of incentive to convince him that Michael had indeed changed for the better, thus creating a means to influence the man's wife to speak highly of Michael in her rounds of gossip.

"I do hope you will have time to speak with me," Michael said. "I will be looking into investing in some new ventures, and I understand that you may have just what I need."

This seemed to excite the Earl, for he gave Michael a low bow. "Thank you, Your Grace. There could be no greater honor."

Of course there would not, Michael thought, *for I have coffers in which you would do anything to place your hand.*

"Excellent," Michael said aloud as he grasped the man in a tight handshake. "I shall speak with you soon." Then he turned to his son. "Come, Samuel, we have business to attend to."

He turned and walked across the street, not surprised to see through a reflection in a window that Lord and Lady Hughes were staring after him as if in shock. However, he pushed the pair out of his mind, for he had others with whom he needed quiet contemplation. Yet, even as he thought on those men who would eagerly agree to completing business with a man of his stature, Michael found that his mind continuously returned to Miss Jane Harcourt, the woman who at this moment was selecting a new gown just for that cause.

For the next few hours, he talked to shopkeepers, bankers, and a host of other people, and his confidence grew tenfold with each passing moment. Few of these people gaped at the scars on his face, many tried to hide their surprise when he walked by, but either way, he simply ignored them. The majority of his time, his mind returned to Jane, and he could not wait to tell her the outcome of this monumental outing.

Chapter Seventeen

Jane had never purchased dresses from such a fancy shop, and she found herself overwhelmed with the entire experience. She had been pushed into a back room, asked to remove her dress, and then one of the assistants had measured her from head to toe, stating that once they completed her measurements, she would be able to choose any dress she wanted and they would be able to make it for her.

Other women in the shop held their head high as they discussed the various gowns and dresses available in the many books that sat on the tables and counters. Jane tried to emulate their looks and movements, but what she ended up with was a stiffness that made her body ache. It took her some time to realize that the best thing she could do was to be herself, for that was the only way she knew.

Although Michael had told her to buy whatever she wanted, she decided that she would select only one new day dress and one gown, for he had insisted on the latter, even if she had no plans to attend the ball. The day dress would be white and the gown would be blue, for that was his favorite color.

"That should do it, Miss," the heavyset woman said as she put away her measuring tapes and made a final note on a pad. "You may return to the front."

"Thank you," Jane said as she redressed and then put on her slippers. When she was finished, she went back out to the front of the shop and began to browse the plates.

A woman walked up and introduced herself as Mrs. Linden, the shop's proprietor. "What kind of dresses are you seeking," she asked as her eyes looked her over with a hint of disapproval. "I'm afraid we do not do burlap."

Jane pursed her lips. Was her silk dress not enough to show this woman that she was not just some simple scullery maid? However, she held her tongue. "I am not certain," she said instead. "I am a governess and I need a dress suitable for day wear and then I need a ballgown."

The woman raised a single eyebrow. "A ballgown," she repeated, the words dry as dust. "And for what would one such as yourself being needing a ballgown?"

Jane felt humiliation rise inside her. If this was how they would be treating her, she would take her business elsewhere. How did this woman know she did not come from at least the gentry?

As if reading her mind, Mrs. Linden said, "That dress is years out of fashion, and I do not have anything similar or doubtless within your budget. You might wish to consider another dressmaker to meet your needs. I believe Mrs. Samson the next street over has options more appropriate to a woman of your...stature."

"Judith?" a woman's voice said from behind her. "What is the problem with my friend?"

Jane turned to find Catherine looking at the dressmaker with a stern expression and felt a sense of relief wash over her.

The dressmaker also looked at Catherine, but it was clear she held no sense of relief. "My Lady," she said with a deep curtsy. "I was merely suggesting that the young lady here..." Then as if realization had hit her, she said, "Your friend, My Lady?"

"Yes, my friend. This is Miss Jane Harcourt and is held in high esteem by the Duke of Hayfield, and she here per his request. Shall I inform the Duke, as well as my husband, that their money is no longer welcome here?"

Mrs. Linden blanched significantly. "No, My Lady, not at all."

"Then I suggest you treat my friend with the respect she deserves."

The woman dropped another curtsy, this one deeper than the first, and then turned to Jane. "I apologize, Miss Harcourt. Now, how may I help you?"

Jane had to stifle a giggle before explaining what she wanted.

"Yes, of course," Mrs. Linden said smoothly once Jane recounted her needs. "Please, allow me to help you with the plates." Jane followed the woman to a counter where several books lay, and she flipped through the pages, stopping on one in particular.

"This is the latest fashion," the woman said, pointing to a high-waisted dress with puffed sleeves and lace collar. "This one would be perfect with your figure. Now, you also mentioned you would like to order a ball gown?"

"Yes, please," Jane said.

Catherine, however, would have none of it. "Nonsense. You must select at least six new dresses and two gowns," she said with a click of her tongue. "You must have several dresses available in case you are invited to tea or some other gathering. And one must not be seen in the same dress on too many occasions."

Jane laughed. "Tea? I have Samuel to look after; I have no time for invitations to tea. Plus, who would invite me?"

"After this grand ball Michael has said he will be throwing, you will be surprised by the number of ladies wishing to spend time with you."

Of course they would, Jane thought. *To collect more gossip.* However, she did not voice her opinion; she would not be in attendance at this ball anyway. Perhaps Catherine was not aware of this fact.

"Six dresses and two gowns," Mrs. Linden repeated with a wide smile. "I will have one of my girls attend to you."

Catherine clicked her tongue in vexation. "With an order of this magnitude, do you not believe it would be appropriate that you attend to Miss Harcourt yourself. After all, she will be putting in such a large order. I would hate to see if she is better treated at Mrs. Valentine's shop."

"No, not at all," Mrs. Linden said hastily. "You are quite right, My Lady; I will take care of Miss Harcourt personally."

"Good. Now, I only came in to see about an order I had placed earlier in the week." When she saw how nervous Jane was, she placed a comforting hand on her arm. "There is nothing to worry about," she said. "The Duke likes his women in the finest clothes. Now, Mrs. Linden will be sure you have the latest styles made of the best fabrics. And you," she pointed to Jane, "will see how much fun it is to shop for new dresses."

And with that, she was gone, leaving Jane to fend for herself. However, the woman's words lingered for several moments, and Jane found herself wondering what she meant when she said that Michael 'likes his women in the finest clothes'.

***

Catherine returned two hours later to check on Jane's progress. It had been a daunting task selecting her new dresses and gowns, but Mrs. Linden had been much more accommodating after Catherine's interjection. Jane, however, continued to be concerned with the number of items she had purchased.

"You seem upset," Catherine said as they strolled down the street. "Was your time at the dressmaker's not pleasant? Do I need to return and give Mrs. Linden a rebuke?"

"No, please, Mrs. Linden was much more helpful after you intervened the first time. Thank you for that." She sighed. "I have been thinking about something and I was wondering if I might ask...What did you mean when you said that the Duke likes his women in nice dresses?"

Catherine stopped and turned to face Jane. "Miss Hester wore the nicest dresses, and that pleased Michael. You see, a man enjoys buying a woman he desires nice things, dresses included. It was just a comment about the general ways of men, nothing more."

Jane worried her lip.

"Did he offer you something more than dresses?" Catherine asked.

"He is a kind man and I do not wish to speak ill of him. However, just this morning he showed me a necklace that belonged to his deceased wife. It held a pendant with blue gems."

Catherine gave a deep sigh and shook her head slowly. "It is as I feared," she said, taking Jane's hands in hers. "Keep in mind that I warned you that this might happen, so please, do as you wish, but be careful."

"I will," Jane promised. "And thank you. I have no one in which to confide, and your friendship means much to me."

"But of course," Catherine said with a laugh. "If you ever need a shoulder on which to lean or an ear into which to speak, I am here for you."

Jane felt relieved that she finally had someone to go to if anything happened with Michael. What she had shared with Catherine had already given her a sense of camaraderie that had been lacking in her life since leaving Anne's tiny cottage, but she still struggled with how to handle her situation with Michael. How could the man offer her jewelry belonging to his former wife? What woman in her right mind would accept such a gift?

Yet, that was where the issue lay—Michael was not in his right mind, was he? No, he was either so disconnected from the real world that he could not see that what he had done was wrong, or he simply did not care. Either situation would be reprehensible, and she wished there were a third option. Unfortunately, the more she tried to find this alternate solution, one would not come to mind.

Frustration raced through Jane. What had begun as a wonderful day had slowly descended into sorrow. Then a peculiar thought struck her. Turning to Catherine, she came to a stop in front of the bank.

"How is it you came to be in town today and then found me so easily?" she asked.

Catherine smiled, but something flickered in her eye that Jane did not like. "His Grace told Robert of your outing today, as well as the dresses he planned to have you order. I must admit that I was curious to see how you would do, and thankfully, I showed up to help you lest you embarrass yourself and the Duke's good name."

"Thank you for your honesty," Jane said, though the barb to the woman's words stung. Yet, what she had expected was a superficial excuse about how she had also wanted to purchase a new dress, so at least the woman was forthwith and honest. However, something tickled at the back of her mind, something that brought her discomfort.

"Now, come. I believe I know where Michael might be."

As Jane followed the woman, her footfalls felt as heavy as her heart. She could not shake the feeling that things were not as they should be when it came to Michael. Perhaps she was naive and refused to see the truth, but she could not shake the feeling that maybe there was more to the Duke's story than she realized.

Regardless, no matter what happened, she needed to take extra care in guarding her heart lest the Duke take it and break it later on.

**

The day had been long, and yet Jane found herself wide awake, sleep eluding her as she thought of the Duke offering her the necklace of blue sapphires that once belonged to his deceased wife. Then her mind turned to his insistence that she purchase new dresses. When she saw the bill that he would receive for her purchases, she thought she would faint, the cost was so high. Perhaps he would faint. She had been too afraid to tell him, and he did not ask, so they had returned to Wellesley Manor, he much too delighted with the progress he had made on the outing to notice how quiet she was.

Samuel, however, took notice of Jane's state of mind and asked after her.

"I am well," she had answered to his whispered question. "I believe that today was just too much for me." Her response seemed to quell his concern, but it did little for her own.

Kicking off the covers, she donned her dressing gown over her nightdress and made her way down to the garden. The house was quiet, all of the servants already abed, likely exhausted from their long day of work. Michael and Samuel would also be fast asleep, dreaming of what each had accomplished during their day in town. Somehow, that thought did nothing for her discomfort, so she pushed it aside and allowed her mind to turn to other things.

Unfortunately, the next topic to spring up was that of Samuel's former governess. Was it true that the Duke had bought Miss Hester an array of dresses and gowns as a means to get her into his bed? The idea seemed utterly ludicrous, but then why had the woman left a position with a child as wonderful as Samuel? Granted, Jane had to leave Arthur due to the Earl's misconduct, but she could not imagine Michael to be such a rogue as Lord Clarkson.

She stopped and sat on a bench that allowed her to look up at the night sky, the stars shining brightly with no moon. She heaved a sigh. No matter what was truth and what was a lie, she could not deny the fact that she cared for Michael as deeply as ever, and yet she feared doing so would be her undoing.

Footsteps on the stone path came to her ears, and she turned to see the man in question approach. He was in his shirtsleeves, the front of the shirt unbuttoned halfway to display a muscular chest. His breeches seemed a bit tighter than usual—not that she took all that much notice at such things, of course—and a wave of heat rushed through her body as she thought of him pulling her into his arms.

She went to rise, but he waved her off. "Please, there is no need to stand," he said in a quiet voice. "I see I am not the only person who is unable to sleep this night. What is troubling you?"

Jane shifted in her seat, not certain how to respond. To mention the dress or the necklace would be much too bold. For the moment, she had no evidence that she should be concerned, although perhaps her own uneasiness should be evidence enough. Instead, she decided to approach the topic of Miss Hester.

"I have been thinking about my lessons for Samuel in the coming week," she said. "It is a shame I never had the chance to meet his previous governess, Miss Hester I believe was her name?"

"It was."

"Well, as it is, I have been curious about how she conducted her lessons."

"I promise you," he replied with a chuckle, "there would be no need for you to worry about that, for you would end up instructing her."

Jane laughed. "Is that so?"

"Oh, very much so." He sat beside her and tilted his head. "Samuel is fortunate to have you."

This man could do no evil, she thought as she wondered if she could ever be in his presence without blushing. However, this still did not explain why the woman left. Even the greatest of rogues could layer his words with more sweetness than candied fruit. "Thank you for saying so," she said aloud. "I forget. Why did she leave?"

Michael hesitated for a moment before he replied. "She had told me that her mother had fallen ill, though I wonder if it was true. I believe it was due to the fact that the rumors surrounding me and my household were more than she could bear, so she no longer wished to be associated with them…or me."

"Rumors?" She wondered which rumors could make a servant leave a position she had kept for more than a year.

He waved his hand in the air as if the gossip was not worth his time. "Oh, most households that employ a multitude of servants must endure such tales, true or not. Apparently, they are true often enough that they are easily believed." He chuckled again. When she said nothing, he turned to her and took her hand in his. "Jane? Has something upset you? You have grown unnaturally quiet since our outing today."

"No," she lied, though she hated to do so. "I am just tired from all the excitement, I suppose. Although I doubt it compares with how the day was for you."

He snorted. "It was quite the experience," he said, and she was glad to have moved the conversation off of her and onto him. "Each moment that passed, I felt my confidence grow. I could not ever imagine feeling so free as I did today."

He had told her about the things he did and the people he met on the return journey, but regardless, she was glad to hear that same excitement in his voice. "I am glad you faced your fears," she whispered and meant it. Jane did not wish to see anyone suffer, but this man even more so. "Your strength is something I admire, and I know Samuel does, as well."

He looked down at the ground and sighed. "My greatest worry is that, as I keep forgetting things, eventually I will forget my son. Or even who I am. Then what will happen? My brother has said he and Catherine would be willing to raise the boy, but I fear…" He allowed his voice to trail off.

Placing her hand atop his, Jane looked into his eyes, darkened by the night. Although the night hid so many flaws around them, she could still see the worry in them, and she now understood why he was unable to sleep.

"You will continue your life as you are now, knowing that I will be with you at your side." She paused. Something bothered her, but she could not quite put her finger on it. "Although, I must admit I cannot quite consign myself to worrying about your mind as you do."

"No?"

"No. I believe we all forget things from time to time, such as when I forgot my gloves earlier. Does that mean that I am going mad? Or is it that I am a woman who, at times, forgets things?"

He smiled and gave her a nod. "Even when I feel the world is pushing against me, your words bring me peace. I find myself once again indebted to you."

Once again he managed to make her blush, and she wondered if he could see the redness of her cheeks in the low light. Then, as if hearing her thoughts, he placed a hand on her cheek, making her breath catch in her throat.

"Your beauty is unparalleled, for you possess a beauty both inside and out."

"You are too kind," she whispered, feeling pulled in by his words. "It is nice to receive your praise, but I insist that you give yourself your proper due."

He moved a thumb across her cheek. "My sweet Jane," he said in a husky voice that made her heart flutter. "The woman who wears the blue dress who captured my heart. I cannot wait to see your new one." Then he leaned in, and as their lips met, Catherine's words echoed in her mind.

"He likes his women in the finest dresses."

Fear overtook her and she pulled back and quickly stood—a mouse uncertain if the cat had seen her.

Michael's face was a bundle of confusion. "Jane?" he asked as he stood, as well. "Have I offended you?"

"No," she said, though her stomach was in knots. Why did he have to say that about the new dresses? Tears stung her eyes as Catherine repeated the words in her mind once again. She somehow felt defiled, her desire for him was so great that his kiss could have led to him to carrying her back to her room, and she would have been powerless to stop him.

"I am afraid that my stomach pains me. I believe I should return to my room and get some rest." The lie left a sour taste on her tongue, as if her body was punishing her for the fib. Without another word, she turned and hurried back to her room, wondering if accepting the dresses would be the start of her downfall.

Chapter Eighteen

The Duke of Fire had been extinguished by the light that was known as Jane, allowing the man, Michael Blackstone, the Duke of Hayfield, to return. There was no other way to explain what had transpired in his life, for he had been a man drowning in shame and guilt until he met her. Now, for the first time in years, he was able to think and see clearly, his future laid out before him in such an obvious way, it was as if a page from a book had come to life. Yet, there was one thing still missing in his life ahead, and he hoped that Jane would want to be an important part of filling that void.

It had been nearly a week since he had kissed her in his gardens, and although she claimed an ill stomach, her face told another story. What he saw in the dim light was sheer panic, fear, and a mixture of emotions he could not comprehend. During the time since then, she had remained polite, even offering him a smile from time to time, but somehow she seemed distant. The separation, though she had not removed herself from his company, left him in a state of melancholy from which he struggled to emerge.

The ballroom, situated on the western side of the manor, glowed from the last rays of the sun as it sat on the horizon. In just three weeks' time, the room would be filled with revelers enjoying music and dancing, as well as food and drink. It had been many years since the room had been used for such a function, and despite the unknown issues with Jane, he found himself anticipating that night. Because the house had been used as a country home, he and Elizabeth had planned to have many parties, inviting all of the *ton* to indulge to their heart's content, and this room had been set up for just those occasions.

138

Although the room was not as large as some of those of his counterparts, the carefully placed mirrors gave it the illusion it was much larger than it was. Paneled walls, mirrors that reached from floor to ceiling, and windows alternated around the exterior walls of the room, that is to say, along three walls. The fourth wall held a set of French doors that led back out into the main entryway. Large candelabras sat in each corner of the room as well as in front of several of the mirrors to allow for maximum lighting. A large chandelier hung in the middle of the room below which Michael imagined groups of dancers working the steps of the latest country dances. The room was perfect and he was glad that it would finally be put to use as it was intended.

When he returned to the sitting room, his mind whirling with images of guests enjoying themselves, he looked up and came to halt when his eyes fell on a portrait of Elizabeth that hung above the hearth. However, it was not the painting itself that made him stop short, but rather the fact that the painting now hung upside-down!

Rage bore through him as he hurried over to the sacrilege before him. How dare someone do such a thing to his lovely Elizabeth!

"Your Grace, I have prepared your riding boots as you requested," Dalton said as he walked into the room. Michael glared at the man. How could he walk into the room and speak as if nothing of consequence had taken place? However, the man had yet to look up from wiping away the last speck of dust from Michael's boots. "Is there another task you wish that I..." He finally raised his eyes and gasped. "Your painting!" the man exclaimed.

"Did you do this?" Michael demanded with such ferocity that the valet cowered before him, his body shaking.

"Never, Your Grace! I would not dare!"

Michael stalked over to the man and glared down at him. The fear on Dalton's face was so pronounced that Michael grimaced. Accusing this man was an unreasonable notion. Why would his valet have anything to do with such a travesty? Why would anyone?

"Let Jenkins know what has transpired here. I want every servant questioned, and when I find out who did this, they will find that their services will no longer be required."

The man, no longer trembling, gave him a deep bow. "As you command, Your Grace," he said. "I will inform him immediately." He turned and hurried out of the room as if he expected the Duke to tan his hide if he did not move quickly enough.

Michael sighed heavily and then returned to stand before the fireplace. Who would have done this? Had he upset a servant somehow to the point that they felt the need to torment him? The idea was ludicrous, not only because he had not heard of any grievances within the staff, but also, the idea to turn a painting upside down made no sense. The act was a show of disrespect to Elizabeth more than himself, and there was none who disliked her in any way.

Then a chill ran down his spine. Had he, himself, done such a despicable deed during one of his bouts of madness? Had he turned the painting and simply forgotten? Yet, that made no sense. He racked his brain for other instances where he had done something like this. There was the time when his banking book had been moved, and to an unlikely place. Other instances popped into his mind, as well. Vases that had been moved and yet none of the maids admitted to moving them. His quill left in the top drawer of his dresser in his bedroom for no apparent reason. One of his cravats tied to the post of his bed.

Frustration raged through him. He could not remember what color coat he had instructed Dalton to bring to him. Just the other day, he had asked that mutton be served for dinner and Mrs. Curtis had prepared venison with the insistence that he had requested it. None of it made sense, however. His mind was as strong as it had ever been, he was certain, and the weakness that had been associated with the Duke of Fire was now gone. So, why would these episodes continue to happen?

He adjusted the portrait and stepped back to admire it. Elizabeth had been a gentle soul, never once an unkind word for anyone; such disrespect was an atrocity.

"Michael?" came Jane's voice from the doorway. "You wished to see me?"

At seeing Jane, his rage dissipated as the light that seemed to surround her fell upon him. If it was not for this woman, he would most certainly have taken complete leave of his senses.

Then a thought came to him. Jane had been upset with him over the past week. Had it been she who had gone into the room and turned the painting? Yet, as she smiled up at him, the thought vanished, much like the sun over the horizon. Jane would never do anything so horrendous to hurt him.

"Thank you for coming to see me," he said as he took her hand and kissed it. "Do you still plan to call on your cousin tomorrow?"

"I would like to," she replied, "unless I am needed here to be with Samuel?"

"No, please. I insist you go and see her. I will be taking Samuel with me out riding for the day. Mrs. Curtis will pack us a picnic lunch and we will go out exploring."

Jane smiled that lovely smile that made his stomach do flips. "He will most certainly enjoy it." She became quiet and it was deafening when coupled with that sadness that crossed her face. How he wished to know what disturbed her so.

"I will see that the carriage is waiting for you in the morning," he said.

She hesitated for a moment and then said, "Michael, I need no such luxuries. I can walk; I am accustomed to doing so, and it is not far."

He did not understand her desire to reject what he offered her. All he wished was to provide the comforts of his station, from a relaxing carriage ride to the purchasing of a new dress and gown. Yet, she continued to show reluctance at accepting them. "Please, I do not like the thought of you walking. It is far enough away that, by walking, you take away some of the time you could spend with your cousin." He took a step closer to her. "Please, you must accept."

Again she hesitated but finally whispered her agreement. Her gaze was on the floor, and he lifted her chin so he could look down at her lovely features.

"I do have one thing I would like to talk to you about," he said as he searched those gray eyes. "Something that is important to me."

"Of course," came her breathy reply. "I am happy to listen and help if I am able."

He smiled down at her and took her hands in his. She did not resist, for which he was pleased. "In just three weeks' time, this room will be filled with people, some, I must admit, I will be happy to see again. Once the last person leaves, only Samuel, you, and I will remain once again. However, we cannot return to what we once were."

Jane gave him a quizzical look. "I do not understand."

"Since you have come into my life, I have never been happier. You know what you have done for me, so here is what I suggest. There is a cottage on this land that I believe would be to your liking."

"You wish me to leave my position?" she asked with a gasp.

"No. Continue to instruct Samuel," he replied. Then he cleared his throat to remove the huskiness that filled his voice. "Allow me to court you as a gentleman should."

He waited for a sign of the happiness he had expected to see on her face, but when it did not appear, worry set in. Perhaps he had scared the woman or had been too forward. "I realize what I ask is unconventional, but courting a woman who resides in my home would not be appropriate. I simply ask you to give me the chance to court you as a man would court a woman, and this was the only option that was sensible."

"Michael, what you have offered me is sweet, but I doubt I would be able to afford to pay for such extravagance."

If this was the cause of her worry, then he had nothing to fear. "I will not ask for rent," he said with a smile. "What I offer you is no different than what I offer you here—that is, room and board. Only rather than having a room within the manor, you will live in a cottage. At the moment, it sits vacant with only a maid who goes out to keep it up. She will continue to do so, even after you have taken up residence." He pulled her hand to his lips and placed a kiss on her knuckles. "Please, allow me the honor of courting you properly and not in hiding."

She glanced down at the floor for a moment, as if considering his words. Then she looked back up at him. "Will you allow me time to consider your offer?"

He nodded. "Of course." Although his voice sounded certain, inside he worried. He had expected her to be joyful in her acceptance, yet that hesitancy was still there.

"I shall retire to my room then," she said as she pulled her hands from his. "I hope your day with Samuel is enjoyable tomorrow." Without waiting for him to reply, she turned and walked out of the room.

Michael knew he would need patience and understanding, for women tended to be strange creatures. His only hope was that whatever he needed to do to make her his for now and for always, he would be able to do it.

***

As the carriage made its way around the drive, Michael gave a slight shake to his head, Samuel silent as his side as they watched the vehicle pick up speed and disappear from sight. Although apprehension still plagued him as he wondered about Jane's thoughts concerning his proposal, he had other concerns on which to focus, the most pressing his outing with his son.

The reasoning behind taking Samuel riding was not only to allow him the opportunity to spend time with the boy, but also to show him the expanse of the lands that one day would be his. He had spent so much of his time closed up within himself, that Samuel had missed out on such experiences that were of such great importance to who he would become.

"I do wish Miss Harcourt was my mother," Samuel said with a sigh.

Michael looked down at the boy with a smile as he pushed back the unruly wave of hair from his brow. "Is that so?"

"Yes, Father," he replied, as if he was imparting great wisdom. "I asked her to be my mother, but she said she could not."

Michael scrunched his brow. "Did she explain why it was not possible?" he asked as they headed to the stables.

Samuel nodded. "She said that one day you would meet a woman and fall in love with her. Then that woman would be my mother. But Father, I want Miss Harcourt as my mother, and you have already met her."

This made Michael smile. Those same thoughts had come his way as of late, but it was not befitting to tell a boy of Samuel's age his intentions, at least not yet. "Miss Harcourt is a very special woman," Michael explained. "However, she is correct; I cannot marry a woman unless I love her, and then I will ask her to marry me. Once we are wed, she will become your mother."

Samuel stopped and looked up at his father. "Do you not love Miss Harcourt?"

The boy's innocence made Michael laugh. "I believe it is time for us to prepare for our ride. We can discuss this another time. What say you?"

Samuel sighed but then smiled when the stable boy brought the horses from the stables. "Very well, I can wait, but not too long."

Michael chuckled. "Not too long," he agreed as he took the reins from the stable boy. He did indeed have strong feelings for Jane, although if it was love, he was uncertain. He had felt the same emotion toward Elizabeth when they first began to court, and that had turned into a love so powerful, nothing could have stopped it. Well, except for the woman's death, and even this his love for her was great.

However, there was no use speculating where he stood with Jane, for he had known that Elizabeth had a great affection for him from the start. If Jane lacked the same capacity to love him as Elizabeth had, then the chances of them developing a true romance could be low. However, if she accepted his proposal to move into the cottage, it would be a great indicator of her feelings for him.

Chapter Nineteen

J ane took a sip of the perfectly brewed tea and relished in the calming effect it had upon her mind. Anne sat across from her at the small table, an occasional grunt coming from the garden as David worked the soil, at times mumbling words that brought a blush to Jane's cheeks.

"That man complains about everything," Anne said with a shake to her head. "Complains about not being home, and then when he's here, he complains about not working. So, I put him to work, and then he complains even more."

Jane laughed as the man of discussion let out another expletive to make a sailor blush.

"Quiet it down, you!" Anne shouted without rising from her seat. "People will think a goat is giving birth!"

Jane covered her mouth in an attempt to hold back another burst of laughter and then wiped tears from her eyes from the effort.

"We should have some bit of peace, at least for the time being," Anne said firmly.

"I find it quite humorous, to be honest," Jane said. "Although, I see even when you tell him off how much you love him."

Anne let out a sigh that held all pretense of some great incumbency. "'Tis true," she admitted. "Although, he snores so loudly he would scare off anyone who would come to do us harm. And he fancies himself a gentleman, which I tell you he is not. But I do love him."

Jane hid a smile behind the rim of her teacup as Anne tapped her fingers on the tabletop. Jane knew that gesture all too well and braced herself for the barrage of questions that were likely to follow.

"Oh, fine," Anne spat as if somehow put out. "There's no spirits in that tea to get you to talk, so it's best if you tell me what's going on rather than me asking."

Jane chuckled. She could never get anything past Anne. "Much has happened since I saw you last," she explained as she set her teacup on the table. "I am not sure where to begin."

"Just tell me what's on your mind, Love," Anne said as she placed a hand on Jane's. "You know you can tell me anything."

Jane smiled. "I do." She took a deep breath and let it out slowly. "I allowed him to kiss me."

Tea sloshed over the edge of the teacup as Anne set it down in front of her, her jaw dropping open. "The Duke of Fire?"

Jane clicked her tongue. "I do wish you would not call him that," she admonished. "But yes, I allowed the Duke to kiss me, and it was the most wonderful feeling in the world." She sighed again. "I have grown quite fond of him, for I have seen the kind soul he hides within him. He is nothing like the rumors say; although there are a few things that have begun to bother me. Then there is his proposal…"

"Proposal?" Anne said. "He asked you to marry him?" She fairly shouted the words, making Jane cringe.

David's voice came through the window. "Who's getting married?" he asked.

"Our mother's cousin's sister," Anne yelled back. "Now, mind your own business." Then she turned back to Jane. "As you were saying, Love." Jane was thankful her voice had returned to a normal volume.

"No, it was not a proposal of marriage," Jane said. "Although he asked me to move into a cottage on his land…"

"A kept woman?" Anne gasped in horror.

"Of course not," Jane said in exasperation. "If you would allow me to finish a sentence, you would have the entire story."

Anne raised an eyebrow at her. "Go on," she said with a theatrical wave of her hand.

"As I was saying, he wishes that I move into the cottage so he can properly court me."

"Then that is a good thing, isn't it?" Anne asked, now clearly impressed.

Jane sighed. "Perhaps. What concerns me is about that which you and another woman have warned me." When Anne gave her an expectant look, she continued. "First, he offered me jewelry, which I refused. Then he insisted that I buy new dresses, which I did. Now, all this talk of moving into my own cottage, courting…I worry that what he wants is to get me into his bed. I have seen this before, and yet I do not feel his motives are the same as what I endured with, say, men such as Lord Clarkson." She gave Anne a beseeching look. "Do you think I am blinded by my feelings for him?"

Anne sat quietly for a few moments before responding. Jane wondered if the woman would ridicule her for being a fool, but instead she replied, "My previous advice to you was meant to protect you, but I see now that it was not the best advice. You are not as naive as I once thought. I take it your feelings for this man have grown if you are even considering his offer?"

"Indeed. Very much so," Jane responded with all honesty. "Being in his presence sends my heart into flutters, and when he takes my hand in his, I find it difficult to breathe. Yet, I cannot help but think that I am a servant, and he is a Duke. You, yourself, have said that such a match cannot be possible."

Anne leaned back in her chair. "That I did," she said with a sigh. "But perhaps I was wrong. Or is it that you are wrong?"

Jane shook her head. "I do not understand."

"What I mean is this. Before, I gave you my warning about men that prey on women for their beauty. But now you say that what has developed between you and the Duke is different."

Jane nodded. "I believe it is, or at least I want to believe it is."

"Then you must confront him and ask him his true intentions," Anne stated firmly. "If you do not, you can only guess what those intentions are, and you may never learn the truth. That is, until it's too late."

Her words sounded a wise counsel and what she said made sense. Perhaps she could speak with Michael and tell him exactly what was on her heart. Yet, as she considered this, a new question came to mind.

"How will I know he is telling me the truth?"

Anne stood and collected the teacups. "The same way you know how

147

you feel about him. Your heart will tell you."

Jane smiled as relief washed over her. Although she did not particularly care for the idea of questioning a man of his position, it was what needed to be done. Furthermore, as Anne had said, her heart would tell her what was truth. And the heart never lied.

***

The following night, filled with both worry and excitement, Jane walked through the doors of Wellesley Manor. Jenkins, the ever-attentive butler, smiled as he bowed his head toward her.

"How was your time at your cousin's?" he asked.

"It was wonderful," Jane replied before glancing down the hallway. "Do you know where I might find His Grace?"

"His Grace is in his library," the man replied as he closed the door behind them.

Jane thanked him and removed her wrap as she made her way toward the library, her heart picking up an extra beat the closer she got. It was time to confront the man and ask him his exact intentions. Simply saying he would court her meant nothing, especially if he was planning to use and discard her. However, she would never allow this man, or any man, to treat her like some common object. She had never permitted it before, and she would not begin now regardless of any feelings she had for him.

When she opened the door—without knocking, she realized with horror, but she pushed the feeling away—and found Michael standing in front of the window, his broad back toward her. She entered silently, and she hoped she did not startle him as she walked up behind him.

"Your presence lights up any room into which you walk," he said without turning from the window. "A feat that amazes me and yet makes me smile every time." He turned to face her and his wide smile almost disarmed her.

She stopped just within arm's length of him, recalling how shocked she had been the first time she had seen the scars on his face. Even today, just as she had back then, she found that face handsome despite its imperfections.

"You are too kind to me, Michael," she said. "I do not deserve such praise." Wishing to change the subject, she asked, "How was your time with Samuel?"

The joy on his face tripled. "It went very well. Samuel seemed to enjoy the outing as much as I."

An awkward silence fell between them, and Jane found herself wondering how she would proceed. She had had the entire conversation mapped out in her mind, but his appreciatory comment had disarmed her.

Perhaps he sensed her discomfort, for he took a half-step toward her, which only increased her discomfiture that much more. Regardless, she had a task to complete, and even the musky smell of his nearness would not distract her from what needed to be done.

"Jane, I feel that a rift has grown between us," Michael said in a sad tone. "I must admit that I am confused. What have I done to offend you?"

Jane shook her head. "You have not offended me," she replied. "It is just that...I need to ask you a question, and I do not wish to make you angry."

He lifted her chin so she was forced to look him in the eyes. "You can never make me angry. Please, ask me anything."

Having him so near brought about a sense of disorientation, so she took a step back on the pretense of smoothing her skirts. She walked over to a chair and placed her hand on its back. "The dresses were a beautiful gift," she said once she was able to produce the words. "Yet I wonder if they are for your pleasure more than for mine." A tear rolled down her cheek, much to her chagrin, and she hurriedly brushed it away before he would be able to see it. "My heart tells me no, but I cannot help but think there is another motive."

"There was a motive behind the dresses," he said, suddenly behind her. She had not even heard him approach, and the feel of his breath on her neck was disconcerting. "I wished to bring you joy and place a smile on your face, for that is what you do for me each time I lay eyes upon you."

She turned to face him, and he was so close that she instinctively leaned back against the chair. "The cottage?" she asked in a breathless questioning. "What are your intentions there?" The air had become heated around them, and she had to grasp her skirts to keep herself from fanning a hand to cool her face.

"To court you properly as a lady should be courted," he said, his voice a light rasp.

"I am no lady, Your Grace," Jane whispered. "At best I am a high-ranking servant and thus do not deserve such treatment."

"You are more than that," he growled. "I care for you deeply. My intentions are pure."

Then she found herself wrapped in his embrace, his lips pressed against hers in a fervent kiss that sent bolts through her body and made her legs grow weak. All worry washed away. It did not matter what Catherine and Anne said, nor what rumors abounded. Had she truly considered those tales, she would have learned that lesson with his recounting of the sad passing of the man's wife. Her heart told her that his words were true, and she knew that she could no longer doubt the man, nor his intentions, ever again.

When the kiss ended, she looked up at his handsome face. "I am sorry for asking such questions," she said. "I know you would not deceive me, so I pray you will forgive me for questioning your motives. I know now that you are telling the truth."

"How do you know?" he asked, a mischievous smile playing on his lips.

"For I care for you," she replied. "It is unlike anything I have ever felt before."

Michael gazed down at her, the desire in his eyes never leaving. "And I care for you," he said. Then he tapped his chest. "My heart tells me the same; that you have no ulterior motives to win my love. So, I must ask you a question, as well."

Ulterior motives? she thought, but his breath on her lips kept her from asking. "And what would that be?"

He took her hands in his. "Will you allow me to court you?"

"I would love nothing more," she replied in a whisper as she wrapped her arms around his neck and surprised herself by pulling him to her for one last kiss.

This time when the kiss ended, Michael pulled away and walked to the fireplace. "After the ball, the cottage will be ready for you. Until then, know that I care for you deeply and that if you wish to ask me anything, never hesitate to do so. For if we hold inside doubt and worry, it will only lead to anger or something much worse."

"I promise I will come to you if I have any concerns," she said as she walked over to stand next to him.

At one point, she had thought him a murderer, but now the notion seemed silly. He was a man of heart, strength, and wisdom, and he brought about a confidence in love she had never known before. She had always admired the looks that passed between Anne and David, and now, she would be able to share that same love with Michael, and the thought excited her even more.

Chapter Twenty

A nd though the sun sets upon this day, I shall remain as the majestic sky, forever."

Samuel looked up at Jane with anticipation. He waited her response to his recitation of a poem he had committed to memory he wished to recite at the ball before he was sent off to bed for the night.

"Samuel," Jane said as she clasped her hands at her breast, "that was beautifully done. Your father will be extremely proud when he hears it."

The boy smiled broadly as he wrapped his arms around her. She returned his embrace just as heftily. "Thank you, Miss Harcourt," he said. "I cannot wait to perform before everyone." Then his eyes went wide. "I almost forgot." He made a bow that, although was a bit unsteady, would have been more than acceptable for a boy of his age before the King himself. Then he pushed back the unruly wave of hair from his brow that always found a way of going astray.

"Well, I believe that, since you have worked so hard, it is time for us to go outside. What do you think about that?"

Samuel nodded enthusiastically, and the pair made their way through the house and out the back door to the garden.

The guests would begin arriving the following morning and throughout the day, and by that evening, the house would be filled. Her heart went out to Michael, who was still busy seeing that everything was prepared and ready before his first guests arrived. He had had very little time to spend with her, but she understood how important this ball was to him.

Earlier she had seen him talking with Jenkins. His gaze had fallen on her and his smile had widened. Even from that distance, she could sense the deep attraction they shared, an attraction that bordered on something else entirely. Although she would have enjoyed focusing on what that 'something else' was, she had a more pressing matter to keep her busy, and it came in the form of a small child who ran freely through the field just outside the garden. The weather was perfect with a bright sun and few clouds to mar his play. They had eaten their midday meal an hour earlier, so she would allow him more time to run and exercise, for the following day he would be confined to the house.

"Miss Harcourt?" the boy said as he joined her on the bench that sat beneath a large oak tree.

"Yes?"

"Why are you not allowed to attend father's party?" he asked with a furrowed brow. "He is going to let Aunt Catherine go." He shook head in disgust. "If she is able to go, then so should you."

Jane smiled and reached over to brush away a bit of grass that clung to his shirt. "Do you not like your Aunt Catherine?" she asked. "She seems to be a very nice woman who cares very much for you."

He looked around to see anyone was nearby and then leaned in conspiratorially. "No, I do not like her, not one bit," he whispered. "I think she is up to mischief most of the time." Jane went to stop him from continuing, but he ignored her. "All she talks about is money. I think she wants my father's money."

Jane clicked her tongue at him. "Samuel, it is not nice to say such things," she said. However, she was curious why he thought as such. "Why do you believe she wants our father's money?"

"I heard her tell Uncle Robert that it's not fair he does not have as much money as Father." The idea of an adult being jealous of another seemed to confound him.

"Well, we should not repeat those things again," she said firmly. "Now, why do you not go and play while I watch you? Let me know how many rabbits you see."

The frown the boy had worn was replaced instantly by a large grin. "I will tell you," he said as he jumped up from the bench. "I bet there will be a hundred of them!" And with that, he ran off toward the small hill.

Jane laughed as she watched him searching through the tall grass, her mind turning to what the boy had said. Although she had seen nothing but kindness from Catherine, she thought back to the night she and Lord Blackstone had come to dine at Wellesley Manor. When Michael had mentioned his desire to host a ball, anger had flickered across her face. Yet, later, she believed that her concern, as well as that of Lord Blackstone, had been for Michael's mental state.

Then a new thought, something she could not quite grasp, tried to enter her mind. However, before it could converge into anything tangible, she looked over to see Michael approaching, as handsome as ever.

"Is all ready for tomorrow?" she asked, although she doubted he had missed even the smallest detail.

"As much as it can be," he replied with a chuckle. "Although there is something important that I have forgotten until now."

"Oh? And what would that be?"

He reached into his coat pocket and pulled out a small card and handed it to her.

Smiling, she took the card from him and read the words to herself.

Miss Harcourt,
It would be an honor if you would meet me in the drawing room tonight at ten.
Sincerely,
Michael Blackstone

Jane found the small gesture endearing and she knew her cheeks had to be a deep crimson. "I accept," she said. She wished to ask him what he had planned, but he spoke before she could do so.

"Until then," he said with a deep bow. "I still have so much to see to." He gave her a wink and then walked away.

Jane played with the card in her hand. Whatever plans he had made for tonight, her anticipation to find out was great.

***

Having already put Samuel to bed some time ago, Jane had more than enough time to ready herself to meet Michael at ten per his request.

Although she did not know what he had planned, the thought of meeting him brought a smile to her face as she looked herself over in the mirror. She had selected one of her new dresses in his favorite color of blue with a deep neckline and lace on the sleeves and banded down the skirt. A large yellow rose had been embroidered on the bodice as well as smaller flowers around the bottom hem. She had to admit, the coloring went well with her complexion, a thought that had never occurred to her before.

She made her way down to the drawing room. The house was silent, for more than likely all of the servants had gone to bed so they would be well rested for the festivities the following day. Even Jenkins was nowhere to be seen, a man who would be in place at the slightest sound of being needed.

Outside the door to the drawing room, she took a deep breath. The candle holder trembled in her hand. Why was she so nervous? she wondered. Perhaps it was the unknown that held her stomach hostage, but whatever the issue, she would never learn what the Duke was up to if she remained in the hallway.

She tapped lightly on the door and then opened it just as the clock struck ten.

Michael stood beside a small table, his dark-blue coat contrasting nicely with the white ruffled shirt beneath it. Just like Samuel, that unruly wave of hair hung over his brow, but he did nothing to push it aside. The rest of his hair was tied back with a dark-blue ribbon that matched his coat.

"Jane," he said invitingly. He lifted two glasses of wine and offered her one. "Surely there is no woman more beautiful than you." He looked her up and down. "That dress displays a beauty I have never seen before."

As was now customary when he showered her with praise about her beauty, her cheeks heated. She closed the door behind her and walked over to him. Although they had shared their hearts, held one another's hands, and even kissed, tonight somehow felt different—somehow special.

"I am graced by your presence," he said.

"The honor is all mine," she replied.

He wore a wide smile. "Tomorrow my home will be filled with guests, all wishing to take a peek at the Duke of Fire. You and I, however, both know that man is now gone."

She nodded. "Indeed. Far gone."

He chuckled. "That is one of the reasons I requested your attendance this evening." He raised his glass. "To new beginnings," he said and then tapped his glass against hers.

"New beginnings," she parroted and then took a sip of the wine. She reveled in the sweet flavor that rolled across her tongue. Never had she tasted such a fine wine.

"Although I wait in great anticipation for the ball tomorrow, I must admit that I look forward to when everyone leaves." He set his glass on the table, and then took hers and placed it beside his.

"Might I ask why?" she asked, although she had an inkling what he might say.

"For I can begin to pursue a woman for whom I care deeply." The words were like honey to her soul, and he grasped her hand in his. "Jane, I will be forever grateful for what you have done for me. When we begin our courtship, I will the happiest man in all of England."

Jane felt her heart soar as she looked up into Michael's eyes. "When I first arrived here, I thought myself plain and unworthy of the admiration of others. However, I have come to learn something of great importance." Her voice was just above a whisper as emotions overtook her heart. "I care not if no one looks at me again, save you. For your gaze is the only one I want because..." her voice trailed off as the realization hit her. Plenty of men who would be considered handsome had cast their eyes her way, but she had not welcomed such infatuation, and she had forced her eyes to down each time. However, she wanted his eyes on her, his smile, the desire alight in his eyes. All of his adoration she welcomed with open arms. Only one reason would a woman ever desire that gaze, and that was when...

"I love you," she whispered.

Michael looked down at her, all that and more in that gaze. "And I love you, Miss Harcourt," he rasped.

This time their kiss was hungry, searching, and she did not want it to ever end. That new emotion, now that it had been voiced, coursed through her, and she now knew what Anne and other women meant by that word.

When the kiss eventually came to an end, Jane laid her head against Michael's chest and listened to his heartbeat as he wrapped his arms tightly around her.

"There is a future for us, Jane," he said as he kissed the top of her head. "I can see it."

Jane let out a sigh. It was just as Anne had said about one trusting their heart. Once again, her heart told her that Michael as telling the truth.

Chapter Twenty-One

The foyer that for years had been quiet—except for servants who passed through or when Samuel came rushing in excited to share his adventures with anyone who would listen—was now filled with voices as lords and ladies talked, their voices carrying over one another. Many Michael had known from years past, but some he had met for the first time tonight. Throughout the day they had arrived, some appearing timid while others seemed fearful as introductions were made. However, their reaction to meeting him did not surprise him, for he knew what they believed of him. Plus, his face did nothing to deter their hesitancy.

Michael wondered if his guests expected a Duke standing beside an open fire acting as a madman might. Perhaps they watched in anticipation for him to show signs that he was losing his mind. A few stared openly at the scars on his face, some with faintly veiled disgust, but most affected not to notice—though he knew they could not have missed them.

In the end, he cared nothing for their opinions or observations, for this ball was not for them. No, it was for him as a way to show all those of the *ton*, from Baron to Duke, that he, the Duke of Hayfield, would carry on as he had six years earlier without fear of ridicule.

"Will we not sit," Robert asked in agitation. "I am growing hungry."

"Not yet," Michael replied. "Jane has planned to have Samuel recite for us first. They should be here any moment."

His brother snorted with contempt. "Surely you do not mean to allow that...servant...to appear before members of the *ton*?"

Michael ignored the man's tone and simply nodded.

"I will tell you this, Michael, and then I will say no more. That woman does not have your best interests at heart. Be careful, for she has somehow charmed you and will seek to find her way into your coffers. Mark my words."

Letting out a small laugh, Michael said, "Your words are properly marked, your wisdom appreciated and noted. Now, let us enjoy this splendid evening before us and not waste such a grand spectacle on something which has no merit."

"As you wish," Robert replied with a bow just short of mocking. "You are the Duke."

"That I am," Michael replied, confidence soaring through him. Then he smiled as Jane and Samuel appeared on the upstairs landing. Samuel looked a smaller version of Michael with his dark coat and trousers and his wild hair neatly combed. His heart filled with pride as he looked at the future Duke of Hayfield, who would no doubt impress everyone this evening with his rendition.

In turn, his eyes went to Jane, and his smile widened further, if that were even possible. She wore her new blue dress, and he knew she wore it for him. Her hair was piled high on her head and blue flowers that matched her dress were woven into her curls. Governess or not, she was the most beautiful woman in attendance, made obvious by the wide eyes of the men and the jealous scowls of the women.

"Your Grace," Jenkins said in a loud voice. "Honored guests. Lord Samuel Blackstone and Miss Jane Harcourt."

Samuel gave a perfect bow and Jane gave a perfect curtsy as the crowd looked on from below.

Michael scanned the crowd and realized that all eyes were on him. "My son Samuel would like to recite a poem before we dine," he announced. Then he gave Jane a single nod.

She smiled and motioned to Samuel to begin.

"The Sun Also Rises, by Michael Turnlow." The boy paused for a moment and Jane leaned over and whispered in his ear. Although Michael could not hear her words, he knew they were words of encouragement, for it was what Jane did—encouraged those around her, having them seek to do their best, and he had no doubt Samuel would do as she asked.

And that he did.

"In the morning, when the sky is not yet light, I take upon my shoulders, the burden of flight. Though I am but a small creature compared to the beast of the land..."

The poem he recited was beautiful, and pride for his son built in Michael to levels he had never known. The boy was articulate and missed not a single beat or word, and Michael's thoughts swung back to the night of the fire and the screaming youngster in his arms as he fought his way through the flames that threatened to take his heir. Now, years later, just the presence of Samuel speaking showed that the fire had lost its battle, at least when it came to his son. Granted, it had taken Elizabeth, and he knew a part of his heart would regret he could not save her, but now a new love had filled that once dark void.

The sound of polite applause filled the room, and Samuel bowed, his grin so grand that it brought about a pleasant laughter. For a brief moment, his eyes caught Jane's, and the pride he saw in them matched his own. One day she would become his wife and thus a mother to Samuel, and he would be the happiest man in the world.

As the applause died off and words of approval came to his ears, he let his eyes linger on Jane for a few moments longer. Her cheeks turned a deep crimson, and he knew her reaction was not a cause of the applause. Since the day she arrived, he wondered how she could tell things about him that he would never have uttered aloud, but now he knew the mystery was now revealed. For when one was in love, no words were needed to express what was on one's heart.

Then he realized that the room had gone to an expectant quiet. "Thank you, Samuel, for your wonderful rendition. And to Miss Harcourt, your wonderful instructor."

Robert snorted beside him as the two turned and headed back from where they had come. They had already dined, and Samuel would be off to bed for the night. Jane had told him that she would retire early, as well, and he wished she had accepted his personal invitation to have her join him. However, just as before, she had declined, outlining once again her reasons a governess should not attend her master's parties.

Jenkins came up to Michael expectantly. It was time for him to announce each couple one by one by title so they could take their place at the dining table accordingly.

A smile came to Michael's face, for in a year's time, he believed Jane would be the first to be seated.

***

Jane sat on the edge of the bed and pulled the thin blanket up to Samuel's chin. Though he had feigned not being tired, the large yawn he let out quickly disproved his claims.

"You see? You are sleepy," she said, and he frowned. "That is fine, though. We all need to rest. You most certainly do, for your recital was so splendid, I believe every person shall be speaking of it for years to come."

The boy smiled. "Do you believe so, Miss Harcourt?" he asked, his eyes so innocent that they warmed her heart. "I think Father was pleased."

Jane brushed back his hair and took his small hand in her own. "Samuel, it was the grandest recital any of my students have ever done. Your father is very proud of you, and I know I am, as well."

"I'm glad we didn't have to eat with everyone," Samuel said thoughtfully. "I think I would grow bored having to bow to everyone. There are a lot of people to bow to, you know." He said this with such authority, that Jane let out a small laugh.

"You are right, I suppose. One day, when you are much older, you will marry and then host your own parties. There will be lots of bowing then."

"That's true," he said with a yawn. "Then one day I will be a Duke. But I promise that if I host a party, you will be invited." He was firm in this statement, and Jane could only smile at his naivety. "I will let everyone know that Miss Harcourt is my best of friends, and she can sit near me."

Jane rustled his hair and then leaned over to kiss his forehead. "That is very kind of you, Samuel. I look forward to receiving your invitation. Now," she said, rising from the bed, "it is time for you to get some sleep."

He sighed as though she requested of him a task so great, the idea of it was simply unbearable. "Miss Harcourt, can I tell you something?"

"Of course. What would you like to tell me?"

161

He sat up in bed as he bit at his lower lip. It was obvious something was bothering the boy. "Would you speak to Father and ask him not to let me go to Uncle Robert's anymore? I don't like him or Aunt Catherine."

Jane scrunched her brow, for this was not the first time the boy had spoken negatively of his aunt and uncle. Retaking her seat at the side of the bed, she patted the pillow and he lay back.

"Now, Samuel, why would you say such a thing? They both care for you deeply and only want to spend time with you."

"You know how you told me it was rude to listen to adults talk? Ease droppings?"

Jane smiled, a shake coming to her head. "Eavesdropping?"

"Yes, that's it. Well, I eavesdropped on them when I was over there last month. Aunt Catherine said that soon my uncle would be the Duke. But that cannot be true because Father is the Duke and there can only be one, I think."

Jane's mind raced as she wondered what the two could have been talking about to bring on such a discussion. The only way Robert would become Duke of Hayfield was if both Michael and Samuel both died. However, Michael's health was fine, and Samuel had many years ahead of him.

When she saw the look on Samuel's face, she reminded herself that he was only a child. Perhaps he had eavesdropped on a conversation mid-discussion, or recalled only bits of it. "I believe there is nothing about which to worry," she assured him. "Your father is the Duke and shall remain so for many, many years to come. Now, do you feel better?"

"I do," he said with another large yawn. "Thank you, Miss Harcourt, you always make me feel better."

"You are most certainly welcome," she said, rising from the bed and picking up the candlestick. "Goodnight and dream of more rabbits."

He laughed and she walked to the door and then looked back at him. The boy was simply adorable, and the thought of one day being his mother made her happy. Closing the door behind her, she thought she saw movement near the Duke's room.

Perhaps he needs to change his coat, she thought as she crossed the hall to her own room. Letting out a sigh, she closed the door, and then a few moments later, began to change out of her dress. She had loved the way Michael smiled at her, his eyes relaying what was on his heart. It was love, pure and simple, but she saw something else, as well—a desire for them both to be together as husband and wife. One day the question would arise and Jane would be required to give him an answer.

As she placed the dress on the bed, a knock came to the door, and before she could answer, Catherine hurried in.

Catherine," Jane gasped as she pulled her dressing gown to her breast.

"Jane, there is no time to talk. The Duke has requested your presence in the ballroom, and I believe he means to introduce you as the one he is courting."

Jane's heart soared as much as it fell. "I do not understand," she said as the woman tried to pull her nightdress over her head. "He told me he wished to wait for him to quell the rumors about the fire before we announced our courtship."

The woman placed her hands on Jane's shoulders. "My dear, there is no time to ponder men and their ways," she said wisely. "Now, fix your hair quickly while I ready your gown."

Jane nodded vaguely and moved to stand before the mirror. Her hair was still up from earlier, but some had come loose with the changing of clothing.

"Now, hurry," Catherine demanded, as if getting Jane out of the room was a matter of life or death. "You must never keep a Duke waiting."

The woman helped Jane into the gown, Jane grateful that she had someone to help her with the multitude of tiny buttons that closed up the back. "Excellent. Now, we can add just a hint of rouge and the tiniest amount of color to your lips." She stepped back to assess her handiwork. "Well, you will not be Queen of the ball, but I imagine all eyes will be on you nonetheless."

Although Jane was directly behind her in the hallway, Catherine insisted on continued speed. "You cannot make him wait," she insisted once more.

As they made their way down the hall, they passed the Duke's bedroom. The door was open and Jane was not surprised to see Dalton inside. Although the candles in the room had yet to be lit, his eyes shone by the lights in the hall, piercing into her as they walked by, and she shivered. What was that man up to?

Well, he is Michael's valet," she thought to herself. *It is no business of mine.*

With hurried footsteps, they rushed down the stairs, the music and voices growing louder with each step. She had warned Michael that it would be best if she did not attend, but he had become much bolder since realizing his worth.

Then her mind turned to Samuel and what he had told her concerning his uncle and aunt, followed by Dalton's sinister gaze, and she cast a glance over at Catherine. The woman wore a crooked smile that bled malevolence.

"Catherine?" Jane said as they neared the ballroom, and she saw Michael standing beside Robert. "Are you certain this is what he wishes?"

Catherine pulled a pin from her hair, shook out several strands and allowed them to fall in a disheveled look. Then she quickly reached out and grabbed Jane's arm so hard that Jane almost screamed in pain.

"It matters not what he wishes," Catherine spat. "It is what I wish that matters."

Chapter Twenty-Two

The ball was progressing perfectly. The melodious music played, drink flowed freely, and the guests danced and laughed. From Barons to Dukes, Baronesses to Duchesses, men and women smiled and congratulated Michael on this, his first ball in a very long time, and although they might still take a second glance when they looked at his face, they no longer grimaced. At least not where he could see. It was a start. Michael made a point of speaking to every guest in attendance so they could see he had nothing to hide; however, he was certain they still spoke behind their hands or off in far corners, but if they no longer openly ogled him, he was making progress. He was not foolish enough to believe that these changes would come about because of the goodness of the hearts of those of the *ton*. He had too much wealth and offered too many business opportunities for them to ignore him any longer. New beginnings nonetheless.

"I must admit, this ball has gone far better than I thought it would," Robert said from beside Michael as yet another important member of society walked away.

"You doubted me, Brother?"

"Not you," he replied, "but your memory."

Michael felt a twinge of sadness. He had hoped to put aside thoughts of his impending madness, at least for one evening, for, as Jane had told him once, "Live for the day at hand and not for the morrow." She always had extraordinary words of wisdom to impart. How he loved her for that.

Robert must have sensed Michael's reluctance, for he did something Michael had never recalled him doing at any time in his life. He apologized.

"I am sorry for doubting you, Michael," he said. It took much for Michael not to gape at the man. "I hope you know that I care for you and Samuel and have only ever had your best interests in mind."

Moved beyond belief, Michael clapped the man on the back. "From the day Elizabeth left me, you have given me great counsel. For that, I am always in your debt."

"You are my brother. If you cannot trust your brother, who can you trust?"

Michael smiled. He did not say aloud that he would trust Jane.

Again, Robert seemed to read Michael's thoughts. "As to that woman. Though it pains me to say it, I must admit that perhaps my suspicions about her were unfounded. I must admit, however, that I still worry about her motives, but I will hold my tongue concerning her since she seems to make you so happy."

"You have no idea how your words comfort me," Michael said with all honesty. Although he wished to share with the man his true feelings—which were beyond happy—he decided to wait. Now was not the time. Once they were officially courting, then he could share with the entire world. However, for the time being, he kept silent.

It was the reason Jane had not attended this evening, and he had agreed it had been the right thing to do. Granted, to have her at his side during such a momentous occasion would have pleased him no end, but the wisdom of her decision had convinced him that what she said was right. Tonight was his night to stand alone, and as to the *ton*, he cared not about what they thought, but soon—very soon—she would be introduced as his fiancée.

"You will see that you were indeed wrong about Jane," he said. "She is a woman of substance with a kind heart."

Robert nodded, but his features expressed some bit of reluctance.

"What must I do to convince you that she is an honest and caring woman?" Michael asked. He gave a laugh when Robert frowned. "Just you wait and see…"

Robert was not looking at Michael but rather was looking past him. "What is going on?" He pointed at something behind Michael. "Look!"

Michael turned to see Catherine stalking into the ballroom, her hair disheveled and her face screwed up in anger. She had Jane in tow, gripping the woman's arm so tightly that Jane grimaced in pain.

"Catherine, what is the meaning of this?" Robert demanded in a harsh whisper. "And why have you brought this...servant...into my brother's ball? Do you not know that you are embarrassing not only me, but him, as well?"

Michael studied Jane's face before turning to Catherine just as Dalton walked up behind her. "Your Grace," he said, giving Michael a deep bow that almost doubled him, "I left to check in on Samuel, and I heard a noise coming from your room. When I saw Lady Blackstone passing by in the hallway, I informed her of what I saw."

Catherine then took up the telling. "That was when I went to the room and I found this *woman* there slipping something into her pocket."

"That is not true!" Jane shouted, wide-eyed and gaping. She gave Michael a beseeching look and shot a glare at Catherine. "I did no such thing."

Catherine spun around. "How dare you call me a liar, *servant*!" She said the word as if it were a bitterness on her tongue. Then she turned to Michael. "I went to confront her and she pulled my hair and attempted to strike me! I have never..." tears rolled down her face as humiliation overcame her, "been handled in such a way!"

Robert went to console his wife. "What did you find in her pocket?" he asked consolingly.

Catherine gave a derisive sniff. "I did not search her, for I did not feel it was my place."

The room had become quiet, the only noise the quiet shuffles of the guests as they strained to see and hear whatever drama was unfolding, much like a pup straining to reach the teat that would give it sustenance. A mortification Michael had never experienced, even after hearing of the rumors surrounding his wife's death, hit him. This could not be true! Jane would never steal from him!

However, doubt trickled through him. What if Robert had been right all this time? Could Jane have been attempting to ingratiate herself into his life in order to get her hands on his wealth?

Michael studied Jane, who had suddenly gone quiet. "Jane, why were you in my room?" he asked quietly.

Tears rolled down her cheeks as she stared at the floor. "I was not."

"Your Grace?"

Michael turned to his valet. "What is it, Dalton?"

"I apologize for speaking out, but Lady Blackstone speaks the truth. I saw it with my own eyes as this woman struck her."

Excited whispers resounded through the room, but Michael ignored them.

Robert stepped forward, his face twisted in anger. "There is only one way to find out the truth and defend my wife's honor, for no one shall name her a liar!"

Michael went to respond, fearing what his brother would do. Before he could take more than a step forward, Robert reached into Jane's pocket and pulled out the very necklace that he had offered her only weeks earlier—Elizabeth's silver necklace with the sapphire pendant.

A collective gasp resonated off the walls.

"I did not put that there!" Jane cried.

"Quiet!" Catherine hissed. "You have been caught red-handed!"

The world began to spin as Robert placed the necklace into Michael's hand.

"Do you not recall," Robert said in a hushed voice, "that I told you how she bragged to my wife about this piece of jewelry? And what of the number of dresses she ordered? I warned you from the very first day I met her that this woman was trouble, did I not?"

Michael felt numb as he nodded. He did remember, but he had ignored his brother's warnings time and time again. Shame and humiliation tentacled through the numbness, soon replaced by hot anger. The woman who would not look up at him, appearing all innocence, but who showed confidence later. Her refusal of the carriage and any gifts he had tried to give. The reluctance to purchase new dresses only to order many. All of that he had dismissed, for he cared for her. He had been foolish to believe it had been because he had convinced her of her own worth when it was all a ruse. Robert had been right all along; she had used him to get to his wealth.

"Jenkins," he said in a cold, firm voice, "escort Miss Harcourt to her room to collect her belongings and then arrange for a driver to send her away from here." Then he paused and added, "The dresses remain. She leaves only with that which she came." He turned to Jane and pushed away the stab of regret that tried to infiltrate his heart. "I trusted you in my home—and with my son. You have broken that trust. Do not ever return."

Robert stepped up and whispered in Michael's ear, "I can send for the magistrate, Brother. Send this woman to prison where she belongs!"

"No," Michael said. "That will not be necessary. All I want is her out of my home...and my life."

"No!" Jane shouted. "Michael...Your Grace, please, do not doubt me! I did not take the necklace!"

Jenkins walked over and grabbed Jane by the arm.

"Goodbye, Miss Harcourt," Michael said before turning his back on her. He could hear the woman's sobs as Jenkins removed her from the room, and he closed his eyes until he could no longer hear her.

When he opened his eyes, he stared into the faces of all of his guests. Many looked away, but most attempted to hide their shock, no doubt filing away all they had seen and heard so they could wag their tongues later. For six years, he had hidden himself away from these people and their harsh gossip. Now that he had built up the courage to face them once again, that courage had been stripped from him all in one night. How would he ever be able to live through his humiliation this time?

***

Never had Jane walked a path of humiliation so great as she did that night as she followed Jenkins out of the ballroom. Casting a glance behind her, Michael still stood facing away from her, any hope of one last look now gone. Not only was her heart broken, but anger swept through her as Catherine gave her a sly smile, half hidden by her down-turned face. Samuel had been right all along; both Catherine and Robert were up to no good. To what extent they had mired themselves into their devious plans she did not know, but she feared for Michael and Samuel.

Wiping at her eyes, she kept her head low. The murmur of voices as the guests spoke in charged whispers rang loud through the foyer as she and Jenkins made their way up the stairs. Once they reached her room, she cast a glance at the butler as he stood with his hands behind him beside the door.

"I do not ask you to believe me," she said. "I doubt anyone would. However, please watch Michael—that it, His Grace—for those close to him seek only to hurt him."

The man seemed to hesitate. Then he nodded. That was enough for her. "I will wait for you in the foyer, Miss Harcourt," he said and then turned and walked away.

She entered the room and closed the door behind her, taking a moment to take one last look at the room that had become her home these past few months. The candle was still beside her bed, its flame flickering and casting shadows around the room. Tears flowed unchecked down her face as she went to the wardrobe and removed the few items she owned, including the old blue silk dress.

She removed the new dress and lovingly placed it on the bed before donning the old one. Although it was no longer in fashion, Michael had said it looked nice on her. At least she would have that memory.

As she added the remainder of her items to her bag, she wondered at how quickly things could change. Just last night, she and Michael had professed their love for one another, and now she was leaving with no chance of ever seeing him again. Throwing her out of his home was one thing, but to turn his back on her publicly told her that he would never trust her or speak to her again. That thought alone hurt worse than anything else that had befallen her this night.

Once her meager possessions were safely packed away, she took one last look at the room that had become her home and wiped away the last of her tears. Life had a strange way of reverse the circumstances of one's life in the blink of an eye.

"You have done very well and will be rewarded accordingly."

Jane turned toward the hushed voice that came from the hallway just outside her door.

"With her gone, our plans can resume unhindered. When my brother has been deemed insane, I will see that he is committed. Then I will step up and take over the Dukedom."

"And a very fine Duke you will be, My Lord. The greatest." That voice belonged to Dalton.

Jane's breath caught in her throat. So, Dalton was involved with this scheme as well as Lord Blackstone and his wife. It all clicked into place as she considered everything that had happened, not only with her but with Michael, as well. Somehow, Lord Blackstone believed he would become the new Duke of Hayfield. However, one person stood in his way. Samuel. Fear gripped her as she considered what that meant.

She held her breath. The voices were now gone, but had the pair continued down the hallway? Uncertainty filled her as she gripped the handle and slowly opened the door.

The hall was empty.

Heaving a sigh of relief, Jane considered her options. She had to somehow warn Michael. However, would he even listen? After all, Lord Blackstone was his brother, and how could he possibly believe that his own brother would plot against him? Jane had only been in his employ for a short time; why should he believe her?

He would not, that was the truth of it.

"Where are you going, Miss Harcourt?"

Jane turned to see Samuel peeking out of his room. She quickly wiped at her face, hoping no more tears shone to upset the boy. "I must go away, Samuel," she replied with a small smile.

"When will you come back? I wanted to show you a new rabbit hole I found, but I suppose it can wait until you return."

She lowered herself to his level. "I will not be returning," she said. "I am sorry."

His lip began to quiver as tears spilled over his lashes. "But you said you would never leave me!" he wailed. "Who will teach me?" Jane pulled the boy into her arms, but he pushed her away. "You promised!"

"Samuel," a voice boomed behind her, "To your room. Now."

Samuel looked at his father and scrubbed at his cheeks. "But, Father…"

"Now!"

Samuel frowned and then turned and ran into his room, slamming the door behind him.

Jane stood and looked around. Seeing no one nearby, she realized that now would be the only chance she had to tell him what she had heard. "Michael, I have something important I need to tell you."

"Nothing you can say will convince me of our innocence. The carriage awaits you out front. Now, go. You have embarrassed me enough; do not continue to add to the shame you have forced upon me in front of people who have finally come to accept me." Then he shouted over his shoulder. "Jenkins, see Miss Harcourt out."

Michael would never listen to anything she told him, and even if he did, he would not believe it. All she could do was leave, so she picked up her bag and moved to walk past him. Then she stopped. "Never doubt yourself," she whispered. He winced but that was the only indication that he had heard her words.

Then she moved past him and followed Jenkins out to the waiting carriage. With one last look at Wellesley Manor, she glanced at the disapproving faces of the *ton* that gazed out the window, more than likely devouring the events that had unfolded before them like a mass of starving animals. However, she cared nothing for what those people thought; only Michael's opinion mattered, and now he no longer trusted or cared for her.

She got into the carriage and the footman closed the door. As the manor disappeared out of sight, she stored away the memories of her time there. They would be held dear to her heart forever. However, they would remain only as memories. Those happy times were now gone and she left just as she had arrived.

Alone.

***

When she stepped from the carriage, bag in hand, Anne came running out of the cottage.

"Jane?" she asked as she took in Jane's wet cheeks and the burden she carried. "What's wrong?"

An eruption of emotions exploded in Jane. "My world," she gasped through sobs that crushed the air from her lungs, "has fallen apart."

Anne pulled her into her arms. "Come inside, Love, and tell me what happened."

Jane had no more fight left in her and she did as her cousin bade, the carriage, the only connection left to the man she loved, riding away, leaving her to face an uncertain life.

Chapter Twenty-Three

It had been ten days since Jane's world had fallen apart, and her heart grew sadder with each passing day. How she missed teaching Samuel and spending time with the young boy, of whom she had grown fond. He had wished for a mother, a role she would have been glad to fill, but that person would not be there.

As for the man who had won her heart, she found that she still loved him despite his anger for her. What bothered her the most was that she had no way to tell him the truth. She had considered writing him a letter to inform him of what she had overheard, but she knew he would not read it. If he did, he would not believe her words. No, what she needed was an opportunity to speak to him face to face so he could see that what she said was true.

These thoughts only increased her sorrow, and she stopped to stand before the window of a dress shop. It seemed only yesterday when she was here and Catherine had come to her aid. How foolish she had been to go against her reservations and allowing the woman to convince her to buy more than the one dress and gown.

However, Catherine had skills that would have gained the appreciation of any playgoer. She had convinced Jane of her kindness, had manipulated her better than any trickster could have. To make matters worse, Samuel had been the only one to see his aunt and uncle for what they were, and Jane had disregarded his concerns with very little consideration. Perhaps if she had asked more questions? Yet, no, she doubted that her opinion would have changed much.

A knock on the window startled her, and Jane looked up to see the proprietress of the shop looking out at her, beckoning her to leave. Beside her stood Catherine, her face filled with smug haughtiness.

Giving Catherine a contemptuous look, Jane moved on down the footpath, though her steps now were more hurried than they had been.

In her hand she carried a package of meat for the evening's meal. Anne and David would be leaving just after noon to visit David's parents, leaving Jane alone at the cottage. Although she enjoyed being in their company, she was glad for the reprieve, for she had had little time alone to think on the events of the night of the ball. Shock still settled on her, not allowing her time to consider what had happened.

Men and women strolled past her, going about whatever business they needed to complete. From time to time, a face she remembered from the ball would come into view, but none even glanced her way, more than likely not recognizing her, for which she was glad.

Then a face that immediately recognized her was before her. Lord Blackstone glared down at her when he almost collided with her as he exited the bank. Evilness poured off him, an almost palpable vileness that left a bitter taste on Jane's tongue.

"Miss Harcourt," the man said pompously, saying her name as if he had bitten into a lemon.

"Lord Blackstone," she replied. She knew she should leave the conversation at that, but her tongue did not heed her mind. "Do not think your conspiracy against your brother will go unnoticed?" If only the acid on her voice could cause him harm.

However, the man showed no sign of distress. "I have no idea of what you speak, *thief*," he said with a chuckle.

This time it was her turn to laugh. "Oh, but you do," she said in a low voice. "I heard you and Dalton in the hallway outside of my room that night, so yes, you do know." She did not miss the flicker of fear in his eyes. "I do not expect a coward such as you to admit his wrongdoing, but I am certain Dalton is not nearly as strong as you."

His face dropped for a moment, and Jane smiled. She might not know how to save Michael from whatever evil scheme this man had concocted, but Lord Blackstone had to know that she would not remain silent.

Lord Blackstone leaned in. "You should be careful of what you say," he hissed in a hushed whisper. "My brother showed you mercy, but I will not."

A couple passed by them, and Lord Blackstone straightened his back and smoothed the anger from his features.

Once the couple was out of earshot, Jane smiled again. "Perhaps he did show me mercy, *My Lord*," she used his title as a curse, "but he is no coward. He is a man of honor, and that is why he will always be a Duke and you only the brother of a Duke." Seeing him wince from the sting of her words was a wonderful reward.

The man took another step toward her, and her heart raced as he stared down at her menacingly, but she refused to step back. She had no doubt he would hurt her, but he would never do it where others could see.

"Why you…"

"Lord Blackstone," a voice said from the doorway of the bank. "What brings you out today? I thought you were leaving for Brighton." A man in a fine coat walked up to Lord Blackstone, giving Jane the opportunity to make her escape.

Jane heard Lord Blackstone give a curt response to the man who had approached him, but soon she could no longer hear their words. She hurried down the footpath toward the cottage, not willing to give the man the opportunity to bully her further.

Although she knew that Michael was a strong man, she worried that his blindness to any wrong his brother might do would ultimately lead him to lose everything he had. Then there was the safety of his heir. What would happen to him when he was the only thing between Lord Blackstone and his goal of winning the Dukedom?

She could not allow the people she loved to be hurt by such diabolical actions. However, the only way she could convey what she knew was to write Michael a letter and hope he would read it, for if she appeared at his door, he would only ask her to leave, just as he had done the night of the ball.

With the words forming in her mind, she hurried her steps, eager for this one chance to warn the man she loved and hopefully save him and his son.

***

It had taken her more than an hour to compose it, several versions strewed across the floor or lay wadded into tight balls. The final copy contained words that came from her heart and soul, and she prayed that Michael would read it and believe what she had written. Whether or not he took her advice and acted upon it was out of her control, but she would sleep better knowing she had done what she could.

As she worked, David and Anne had packed what they would take with them on their journey, and they agreed to take the letter to Wellesley Manor on their way.

"Anne, I do not know how to thank you for doing this for me," Jane said, handing her cousin the letter she had painstakingly written.

"'Tis no bother, Love," Anne replied as David called out from the front of the house. The woman turned and shouted, "I'll be right there! Have patience!" Then she turned back to Jane. "I'll drop this by straightaway. Hopefully he'll see what you say is true."

"That is what I hope," Jane said with a sigh. "Even if he does not believe me, perhaps he will begin to question his brother's motives. If even that happens, I will be happy."

Anne placed a hand on her shoulder. "You are a good woman, Love, and deep down in his heart, he knows that."

David came to the door, his face red and his breathing heavy. "The horses are ready and so am I," he grunted and then headed back out.

"We will return next week," Anne said and then gave her a hug.

"Have fun and enjoy your visit," Jane said.

Anne rolled her eyes and lowered her voice. "With his parents, I doubt that will happen."

Jane giggled as she followed her cousin through the front room and out the door. She watched as they got into the buggy, David complaining about the receding sun, even though they had plenty of time to get to his parents' home before the sun set. With a wave, the pair were off and soon they were out of sight.

Jane sighed as she closed the door and offered up a prayer that Michael would heed her words, for his life, and that of his son, depended on it.

The Duke of Fire

Chapter Twenty-Four

Michael walked along the garden path with his son Samuel by his side. Although he smiled at the boy as the two conversed, inside he felt anything but happy. In fact, he was crestfallen. No matter how hard he tried, he could not eliminate the images that continuously played in his mind the events of ten nights prior, when he had sent Jane away. The moment the words left his mouth, a part of him inside died. A light had gone from his world, a beautiful light that only she could provide.

Of course, anger for her transgression still coursed through him. How could she have stolen from him? Even worse, how could he have trusted her? Although he loathed to admit it, Robert had been right all along. Since Elizabeth's death, all counsel Michael had received from his brother had been valid. Yet, on this matter he had ignored his brother's pleas to remove the woman from her position. Now he was paying the price, if not in a financial capacity, certainly within his heart.

"Father?" Samuel said as they reached the far end of the garden. "I wish Miss Harcourt was here."

Michael looked down at his son and placed a hand on the boy's shoulder. "I understand, but I have put out adverts to find you a new governess. Do not worry, you will be back to your studies in no time."

Samuel frowned. "Why can Miss Harcourt not return? She made me happy."

Michael nodded, unable to voice that she had also made him happy. How could he tell the boy that the woman who he saw as a replacement for his mother had stolen from him and that she had only used them both to get into Michael's good graces? Such words would only crush the boy and would serve no purpose. At least, not until the boy was old enough to understand.

Therefore, Michael replied in a different way. "Oftentimes people must leave to conduct other business. Remember, I was her employer, so she was paid to complete the requirements of her position. Sometimes other opportunities arise and they must change their plans. Miss Harcourt did not wish to leave, but circumstances led her to do so." Granted, what he said was not an outright lie, but it was very nearly close.

Samuel seemed to consider Michael's words and then he nodded.

Michael ruffled the boy's hair. "Now, go and play for a while."

"Yes, Father," Samuel replied, though he did not run as he once had.

Michael sighed. The boy no longer carried the glow of happiness he once had, but there was nothing Michael could do about it. Children were resilient, so once a new governess was found, everything would return to normal.

His mind returned to Jane and that fateful night. It made no sense for her to steal what he had offered her as a gift, especially on that particular night. Perhaps she saw an opportunity to take the blame off herself while the house was filled with guests.

Walking over to a bench, he took a seat as Samuel began poking at the ground with a stick. Michael's thought continued on their journey. The night before the party, she had confessed her love for him and his for her. He thought he had read the truth in her eyes, but had he wished it to be true to the point that he saw only what he wished to see?

Frustrated, he rubbed his temples. She had placed blame on Catherine for what had transpired, but what could Catherine hope to gain by having Jane dismissed? She had nothing to gain by such a tactic, and he could see no motive. Catherine had always been a kind and polite woman who had taken a great fondness to Samuel. The more he dwelt on it, the more he felt his mind falter. Perhaps all his thoughts stemmed from a failing mind.

"Your Grace?"

Michael turned to see Jenkins standing stoically behind him, a letter in his hand.

"Thank you," Michael said as he accepted the letter from the butler. He slipped a finger under the wax, unfolded the paper, and began to read the careful script.

Dearest Michael,
I know you are angry with me, but I beg you to listen to what I have to say. It is with great regret that I inform you that your brother and his wife, along with Dalton, are conspiring against you to convince you that your mind is not as strong as it should be.

He laughed aloud and placed the letter on the bench beside him. He would not listen to the rantings of a woman who would deign to steal from him. How could she expect that his brother would be conspiring against him? To what end?

Picking the letter up, he went to tear it to pieces as a final act of shutting Jane from his life forever, but he found he could not do so. Instead, he found himself reading her words once again.

You are not going mad. I do not know how, but they have convinced you that your mind is gone, or at least in the process of going. Please, do not listen to what they say, for your brother wishes to see you declared insane so he can take over your title and estate.

The more he read, the greater his anger grew. To what lengths would the woman go to try to win him back? Apparently to any.

Doubt me until your last breath if you wish, but ask your son what he knows about the scheming his aunt and uncle have done. I know you would not doubt his words.
With love,
Jane

What would Samuel know about the conspiracies of his elders? He was only a child. Surely she had not convinced the boy to lie?

Gripping the letter in his hand, Michael called out to Samuel, who came running over as he threw his stick aside.

180

"Samuel, come sit beside me," he said as he attempted to keep his voice level. He had no cause to become angry with the boy.

Samuel did as his father asked. "What is it, Father?" he said, concern written on his face. Perhaps Michael had not hidden his irritation as well as he thought.

"I wish to ask you something, and it is imperative you are honest with me. Do you understand?"

Samuel nodded. "Of course," he replied, as if he would never consider lying to his father.

"You know I am the Duke of Hayfield?" he began, and the boy nodded. "Do you have cause to believe that someone else would like to be Duke of Hayfield?"

"Oh, yes," Samuel said with surety. "Uncle Robert does. I ease dropped...I mean eavesdropped him telling Aunt Catherine when I was at their house."

Michael studied his son's face. Was the boy lying? Perhaps he had misunderstood a comment Robert had made in a jealous rage. He ruffled the boy's hair. "Thank you, son. Now, I want you to go play for a while longer while I attend to some important matters. I will come for you soon."

"All right, Father," Samuel replied as he stood. Then with a wide smile, he took off running, grabbing the abandoned stick as he ran past it.

Michael walked to the house. Could it be true that Robert and Catherine, along with Dalton had been contrived a scheme to convince him he was losing his mind? The idea seemed ludicrous, but the more he thought on it, the more events fell into place.

"Have Dalton come to my study," Michael said as he passed Jenkins in the foyer.

The butler bowed. "Yes, Your Grace."

Michael did not wait to see if the man did his bidding but hurried to his study. He went straight to his desk, took out a slip of paper, and wrote a single word on it. Then he folded it and placed it in a drawer.

Dalton came in moments later, giving Michael a diffident bow. "You called for me, Your Grace?"

"I would like you have my blue coat ready for me for by seven. I will be going out for the evening."

"Yes, Your Grace," the man replied and then hurried away.

Michael pulled the paper from the drawer, read what he had written, and then returned the paper to the drawer, locking it with the key. Soon he would finally learn if he was truly going mad.

***

With a cup of tea in her hand, Jane stood outside of the tiny cottage looking up at the stars. Night had descended upon the world an hour earlier, and all lay quiet. Her mind turned to Michael and the many nights they had stood beneath such a sky, standing hand in hand as they gazed up at those tiny lights. Simply being in each other's presence was fulfilling, and she dearly missed the closeness they had shared. For at least the hundredth time, she hoped he had read her letter and then perhaps had set out to come and call on her. However, as each minute ticked by, she began to doubt he would make such a trek.

After all, he saw her as a thief, and to think a man of his station would come to her after what he believed she had done made her feel a bit childish. She imagined him walking up the short path that led to the cottage, a smile on his face as he pulled her into his arms. Then he would listen to her tell of what she had overheard in the hallway that night—that Lord Blackstone was out to hurt him and that she only wished that he and Samuel were safe.

She sniffed at the absurdity of her thoughts. Why would a Duke listen to a governess? No, a former governess. A servant. There was her answer. He would not, and that was that.

With a sigh, she went back into the house and placed her empty teacup on the counter. If only he would consider her words, he would see the truth in them. Yet, if someone came to her and accused Anne of such heinous acts, would she believe him? In all honesty, she doubted she would.

She removed the blue dress, hung it on a peg, and went to the bedroom. Sliding beneath the covers in only her shift, she laughed thinking of how she had tended Michael when he was ill and how he had carried her to her room, she so tired that she could only nuzzle up against his chest. It seemed like years ago as she recalled the feeling of safety while in his arms.

Sighing, she snuffed out the candle and lay back. Yet, however much she tried to redirect her thoughts, imagines of Michael returned. She still loved him and always would, but she prayed he loved her enough to listen to sense. Her eyelids became heavy, and soon dreams of him riding up to the cottage played in her head. He would pull her into his arms and kiss her as deeply as he had before when he realized that all she had said was true.

The snort of a horse roused her from her dreams, and when someone knocked on the door, she leapt from the bed and hurried to answer, joy raining down on her. He had come!

She unlatched the door and opened it wide, but it was not Michael that stood there, but rather Lord Blackstone.

"No one threatens me!" he seethed as he reached out and grabbed her throat.

Jane tried to cry out, but his hand squeezed tighter, cutting off any sounds she tried to make. She brought her hands up and clawed at him, but his grip was so tight that she could not break free. Pinpricks of light danced behind her eyelids, and she was reminded of the stars she and Michael had enjoyed. Her legs grew week, and fear grew inside her.

"You will meet the same fate as Elizabeth," he spat as her eyes struggled to keep focused. "Killing a servant will be much easier than killing a Duchess."

***

Jane opened her eyes to find her hands bound behind her and a rag stuffed in her mouth, tied off with a piece of cloth. Her mind raced as she recalled Lord Blackstone grabbing her by the throat. Yet, why had he not killed her? Fear coursed through her when she turned her head and saw the man who had accosted her squatting down beside the fire that burned in the hearth. In his hands he held a long stick, which he used to stoke the flames.

183

"I see you have awakened," he said with a villainous smile. He walked over to where she lay on top of the table. When she cringed, he let out a deep laugh. "You should have kept away from my brother like I asked you. But no, you had to try to save him."

She tried to scream, but it only came out as a muffled sound, the rag blocking her voice. Lord Blackstone only laughed that much harder as he returned to the fireplace and pulled out the now burning branch from the fire. Walking over to the curtains, he touched the flames to the fabric, and they were ablaze in seconds.

"Once the roof ignites," he continued as he walked to another window, placing the burning branch to that curtain, as well, "you will only have moments to live. If you are lucky, you will die long before then. But if I am lucky, I will hear your screams from miles away." He leaned in and kissed her cheek. "Goodbye, servant." Then he walked out the front door leaving Jane to her fate.

Jane panicked and swung her bound legs over the edge of the table. She hopped a few paces before losing her balance and landing on the floor, what little breath in her chest forced out. The flames had engulfed the curtains and now ate their way along the walls, leaving a haze of smoke in their wake, making it difficult to see. Tears rolled down Jane's face and she attempted to cough and remove the smoke that filled her lungs she had breathed in through her nose, but the rag made it impossible to expel the poisonous fumes.

How she wished that Michael was there so she could tell him how much she loved him, but he had not come. All she could do was hope that her letter had conveyed her thoughts completely and that he and Samuel would be safe.

As the minutes ticked by, the flames and smoke increased, creeping closer to where she lay. Her vision became blurred as breathing became almost impossible, and the last thought before she passed out was how much she loved Michael, and that she hoped he would not blame himself for her death.

Chapter Twenty-five

Michael stared at the clock on the mantel and watched as the hands shifted with the passage of time. In only a few minutes, it would strike seven, and he would learn the truth, or at least a part of the truth. By all accounts, he appeared relaxed on the outside, but inside he was a pot of boiling water. The more he considered the events that led up to the party, the more he began to doubt his brother's intentions. Could Robert have truly been conspiring against him? He trembled at the thought. Yet, after reading her letter, he found that what she said made sense. Furthermore, he could no longer doubt her after what Samuel had revealed. For a moment he thought he would rather be going mad than to believe that his brother would cause him harm.

Regret filled him as he thought of that night and he having her thrown out of the house. How angry he had been when he should have been listening to what she had to say. However, he could not dwell on what had already transpired; no one could change the past.

The clock struck seven as the last rays of sunlight disappeared over the horizon. No candles had been lit, and the dusk that filled the room would benefit his purposes perfectly.

"Your Grace," Dalton said in the doorway.

"Come in," Michael said as he stood, though he remained behind the desk.

"Your coat," Dalton said as he raised a dark garment toward Michael. The color of the coat the man held in his hand was obscured by the semidarkness, which was exactly as he had hoped.

"Light the candles," Michael commanded.

Dalton gave him a confused look but laid the coat over his arm and proceeded to do his master's bidding. When he was done, he once again held out the coat, the black of the material unmistakable in the brighter light of the glowing candles.

"Did I not ask for the blue?" Michael asked with an attempt to keep his tone as even as he could.

"Forgive me, Your Grace," Dalton said as he gave Michael a bow, "but you had requested the black. However, if you would like…"

"No. I will use the black. You may go."

Dalton bowed low, draped the coat over the back of a chair, and then left the room.

Once the man was gone, Michael dropped into his chair and stared at the fire as he collected his thoughts. He removed the key from his pocket, opened the drawer, and took out the scrap of paper. With trembling hands, he unfolded the paper and took a quick intake of breath.

"Blue."

Jane had told the truth about Dalton. This meant that whatever else she had said was more than likely truth, as well. What he needed to do next was to find her and talk with her.

Hurrying over to the door, he called for Jenkins, who came rushing from the dining room, a silver fork still in his hand.

"Your Grace?" the man asked, concern etched on his face.

Michael stopped. What part had this man had in his brother's scheme? he wondered. Yet, Jenkins had been with him for years, not once offering a single complaint. Nor had he ever insinuated that Michael was struggling with his memory.

"I will be leaving very soon," Michael said. He had to trust someone. "Send a rider to my brother's house to tell him he is needed here immediately." Then he lowered his voice so that only Jenkins could hear. "If Dalton tries to leave this house while I am gone, I know you will do everything you can to see that he does not. Am I correct in saying so?"

"With my life, I will stop him."

Michael clasped the man on the shoulder. "Very good. I am off." He opened the door and hurried out into the night. His brother would regret ever making him doubt not only himself, but the woman he loved, as well.

***

A bright glow lit up the sky toward the east as Michael made his way down the road toward the house belonging to Jane's cousin. There he would find Jane and apologize to her for not believing what she had tried to tell him. She had done nothing but care about him since she first arrived at Wellesley manor, and he had let her down by not heeding her warnings. Well, he would rectify that problem this very night.

As he came around a curve in the road, the strange glow intensified, and he realized that what he was seeing was the glow of a large fire. He pressed his heels to the flanks of his horse and urged it to a run. When he got to the path that led to the cottage, his eyes widened in fear when he saw the flames that danced on the roof.

He was off his saddle before the horse came to a full stop and racing down the path, hurtling over the gate as if it were barely there. Flames shot out from one of the windows, but the structure was still sound. If Jane was in there, the chances of her still being alive were thin, but he could still have a chance to save her. He would not lose her like he had lost Elizabeth.

"Jane!" he yelled. He listened for any response, but none came, and his heart sank. "Jane!"

He had to see if she was inside. Making his way up to one a window that was still intact and looked inside. The room, a bedroom by the looks of it, was filled with smoke, but the door was open into the main room. He searched as much as he could for any sign of Jane or her family, but he could find none. Then his eyes fell on two feet, soles up as if the person to whom they belonged lay on the floor on his or her stomach. That meant that at least one person was in the house.

Using his elbow, he broke the window pane and then cleared away as much of the glass as he could. Then he crawled into the room, the remnants of the glass tearing at his coat. Crawling on his hands and knees where the smoke was thinner, he made his way to the main room. There, the smoke was thicker and heat singed his hair, but lying on the floor just inside the room was Jane.

He loosened his cravat, pulled it over his mouth, and crawled to Jane's side. She had a piece of cloth tied around her mouth and her feet and hands were bound. How could anyone have done this to her? He felt her back and was relieved to feel the faint movement of her breath. Then he heard a familiar creak above him, and his mind momentarily returned to that night six years earlier. Panic overtook him and he thought he would collapse, but as he looked into the face of the woman he loved, he knew he could not die, for if he did, so would she.

"You will not win this time!" he shouted to the fire that surrounded him. Smoke entered his mouth and he coughed as he pulled the cravat back into place. He pulled Jane into his arms, and the heat intensified as he pulled her close to protect her against it. As he turned to make his way back to the bedroom, the roof came tumbling down, blocking their escape. However, he refused to give in to the inferno this time, the fire that wished to finish the task it had failed to complete the first time. Instead, he looked around until he found a path that led to a door. He only hoped the door led outside.

Lowering his head, he pulled himself and Jane along the floor, the flames flickering toward him as if to torture him. Yet, he continued. Once again, the roof creaked, and he glanced above him. If he did not get out soon, they would both be dead. Bowing his head, he continued his trek, and his head hit the door before he realized he was there. With one last burst of energy, he pulled the door open and pushed Jane outside.

He crawled into the night air, pulling Jane across the grass just as the remainder of the roof fell in. Then he collapsed on the ground, pulling in gasps of fresh air and coughing out smoke. He sat up and turned Jane over, fear coursing through him that he had been too late, or that he had not moved quickly enough. Her skin had spots of black but he could see no other damage. Yet, she lay motionless before him.

"Jane, my love," he whispered. "I am so sorry for having doubted you." Tears filled his eyes as regret tore through him. If the woman died, it would once again be his fault, and then he *would* go mad. "I love you."

The only sound was the crackling of the fire behind him as he leaned over and kissed her. When he moved away, he saw clean lines where his tears had fallen on her soot-covered cheeks.

Then she coughed, and joy rushed through Michael as he brushed her hair from her face. After several harsher coughs, her eyes fluttered open and she stared up at him. A light shone from her eyes, and he vowed it would remain there forever.

"Michael," she said in a croaking voice, "you saved me from the fire. I...knew you would come." She closed her eyes and leaned against his chest.

"Yes, my love, I did," he replied. Then he picked her up and carried him to his horse. He glanced down at the woman in his arms and then looked back up at the flames that were dwindling. Like the remains of that cottage, the Duke of Fire, and his guilt, were now nothing but a pile of ash.

Chapter Twenty-Six

Michael sat on the edge of the bed where Jane lay sleeping. The only sounds coming from her were a few hacking coughs and a wheezing from deep in her lungs. As soon as he had ridden up the drive to Wellesley Manor, Mrs. Fredericks, the housekeeper, had immediately taken charge, sending off one maid for warm water and another to find as many clean cloths as she could find. He had insisted in washing the soot from her face and arms, much to Mrs. Fredericks' shock and horror, which the woman quickly quashed in equal horror that she had reacted so to a Duke.

However, once the water and cloths arrived, Mrs. Fredericks sent Michael from the room so she could see to Jane being washed. Apparently there was a limit to what she considered allowably proper.

"It is one thing to have a Duke seeing to a woman in his household, and quite another to have that same Duke taking the liberty of seeing said woman in a manner that all too inappropriate in polite society." Her tone held admonishment as she spoke, even as her eyes held sympathy. It was not as if Michael had hidden his feelings for Jane from those around him, and clearly the housekeeper either approved of their association or simply sympathized with his suffering because he was Master of the house. Whatever her reason, he welcomed it wholeheartedly. At the moment, he would take any support from wherever it came, though he would never admit such weakness aloud.

The entirety of his wait had been spent in pacing the hall in front of Jane's door, his mind churning over the events of the night. How had she come to be tied up? This fact pointed to an assailant of some sort, someone who wished her dead. But who would want such a thing of a woman such as Jane? Did she have any enemies who would go to such lengths?

At times, his thoughts ran wild. *Was it coincidence that Jane's cousins had not been at the cottage while their home burned?* Then, when he had laughed at the absurdity of those thoughts, he realized that there was a good chance that the couple had no idea that their home had burned to the ground. Had they returned to find everything they owned beneath the dying embers of their home? Or were they on a long journey without one thought of what wait for their return? Would they wonder what happened to Jane?

The door to Jane's room opened and one of the maids bobbed him a curtsy. "Mrs. Fredericks says ye can go in," she said before bobbing another curtsy.

He did not wait for the girl to move aside and almost trampled her in his rush to be with Jane.

"She'll need time to recover, Your Grace, but she will live," Mrs. Fredericks said. Then she looked down at Jane as a mother would a child. "She just needs rest." Then she called the maid to her and the two were soon gone, leaving Michael alone with the woman he loved.

Jane coughed, her hand covering her mouth, and Michael rushed to pour her a glass of water. He brought the glass to her lips and she took a sip before pushing it away.

"Jane," Michael said in a quiet voice as he pulled a chair up next to the bed and took her hand in his, "can you tell me what happened?"

Tears leaked from the corner of her eyes, and at first Michael thought she would not speak. However, her eyes fluttered open, red and swollen. "It was..." Another fit of coughing had her doubled over for several moments. When she was done, he offered another glass of water.

She shook her head. "No more," she sputtered. Then she lay back against the pillows and looked up at him sadly. "It was...Lord Blackstone. Your brother."

The air around him seemed to vanish and he found himself fighting for air in much the same way as he had in the burning cottage. The room spun around him for a moment, but when he saw the anguish in Jane's eyes, he caught hold of his senses. She had suffered enough; he could not have her endure more while he attended to his grief. For grief was what he suffered. His brother was as good as dead.

"He will pay for what he has done," he vowed in a quiet tone he knew held an edge sharper than a knife.

Jane grasped his arm and her eyes bore into him. "That is not all," she rasped. The racking cough once again had her doubled over, and it took several moments to subside. She accepted the water he offered her but only enough to wet her throat before pushing the glass away. She did not settle back into the pillow this time but squeezed his arm weakly to keep herself in a half-sitting position. "Michael, Robert killed Elizabeth. It was he who set the fire that left her dead and almost killed Samuel."

If the world lurched around him before, this time it spiraled out of control. The man in whom he had put all trust had been the one who had made him suffer the worst tragedy any man could endure. Michael would see that man pay for what he had done. Not only to Jane, but to Elizabeth with her life. And Samuel with the loss of a mother he would never know.

"Rest, my love," he said, every muscle in his body tensed to maintain an outward appearance of calm. "I will return later to see how you are feeling, but for now, you only need to rest. I will take care of all the rest."

Jane nodded and closed her eyes, the even breath of sleep on her in seconds. Michael laid a hand on her brow and then leaned over to kiss her cheek. "I will see everyone I love avenged." The promise came as a whisper.

***

Michael stormed down the hall and stalked to the study to pace before the fireplace. A rage greater than the fire in the hearth coursed through his veins as he grasped the decanter of brandy. Then he turned and threw it against the far wall and watched as the amber liquid streamed down the dark wood.

The door opened and Jenkins entered. Before the man could speak, Robert burst in behind him, his features indignant. "What is the meaning of having me pulled from my bed in the middle of the night? What is so urgent…?"

Robert's jaw cracked as Michael's fist smashed into it, and the man flew back into a chair, which overturned from the blow. The man barely had time to pull himself up and shout, "What is going on?" before Michael had him by the collar and was pulling him to a standing position.

"You killed Elizabeth," Michael seethed as he pulled his brother to him so their noses almost touched. "You tried to kill Jane." His voice was as tight as the fist at his side. "Why?"

"I have no idea…"

Michael's fist crashed into his brother's face again, this time leaving the man's nose askew. "Why?" he demanded again, a spring ready to uncoil.

Robert glared at Michael, ignoring the blood that gushed from his nostrils. "That woman was not worthy of the title of Duchess." He spat more than what Michael suspected was blood. "My Catherine is more deserving of that title than that stupid woman ever could have wished to be." His face pinched in disgust. "You always had a soft spot for people beneath you."

Michael narrowed his eyes at the man he had once thought of as his brother. "I have every right to choose whom I marry," he said.

Robert snorted, or at least attempted to through his broken nose. "I should be Duke, not you!" he sneered. "You might be the elder, but you have done nothing to earn the title. I, on the other hand, have done everything. If it were not for me, you would have watched as the estate, all the lands, even the wealth dwindled away. All because of a woman! You had eyes only for Elizabeth and I saw the devastation you would have left behind, the neglect. You have never been worthy of Father's title, and you never will be." Then his face twisted into something so ugly, Michael almost took a step back. "And that brat of yours?" he hissed. "He is as weak as you."

Michael's fist slammed into the man's face again and again, and he did not stop until a voice behind him halted his hand.

"Father?" Michael turned his head and looked at his son, whose face was contorted in horror. "Father, please, do not become him," Samuel said as tears ran down his cheeks. "If you do, the darkness that left this house will return."

The boy's words, a proclamation that held meaning even men struggled to comprehend, struck Michael with such force, he wondered if his son had doubled up his fist and struck him. He looked down at the battered face of his brother and released his shirt, pushing the man to the floor. "Bah!" he shouted. Then he turned to Samuel and knelt before him. "You are wise beyond your years," he said and then pulled the boy into his arms. "I am so proud of you."

When the embrace broke, Michael rose. Jenkins stood at the door, a silver tray gripped in his hand, still raised as if he meant to strike someone with it. "Jenkins," Michael whispered as he grasped the man's wrist.

The butler seemed to come around, as if his mind had been far away. He cleared his throat, his face turning red from embarrassment. "Your Grace," he said with a deep bow. "Forgive me. I heard what...*that man*...did to the Duchess and I am afraid I lost my head."

Michael chuckled. "As you can see, I lost my head, as well." Then he pursed his lips. "Send a rider for the magistrate. I want someone here to collect him," he pointed to Robert who lay unmoving on the floor, "and I want another man to go collect Catherine. I care not if they must tie her hand and foot, I want her treated like any other criminal who has conspired to murder."

"As you wish," Jenkins said stoically, although a corner of his mouth rose for a fraction of a second.

"One more thing. Where is Dalton?"

Now Jenkins did chuckle. "He is tied up in the kitchen being watched over by Mrs. Curtis, Your Grace. She caught him attempting to slip out after you left." A moan came from the man on the floor. "And what will you do with him?"

"Let him be," Michael replied. "If he decides to run, allow him to do so, for everyone will know of his deeds. He has no place to hide." He walked up to his son, picked him up, and placed a kiss on his cheek. Then he pulled him in and held him tight. "Things will change from now on, I promise," he whispered.

"Good," Samuel whispered back.

Setting Samuel back on the floor, Michael took the boy's hand in his and walked out into the foyer.

"Where are we going, Father?" the boy asked.

"To see Jane," replied Michael.

Chapter Twenty-Seven

*F*ire and smoke filled Jane's dreams, as flames jumped out at her and morphed into images of Lord Blackstone towering over her as he cackled with madness. She looked down at the cords that bound her hands and feet and quailed as they burned away, expecting her skin to be a charred mass by the end.

Jane's eyes flew open and she gasped before realizing she was in her bed and the only flames that burned were in the fireplace. Her heart leapt with joy when she looked down to see Michael's large hand holding hers.

"Michael," she said and was surprised how rough her voice was.

He sat up in the chair where he had clearly fallen asleep. Dark circles rimmed his eyes and his face looked haggard, but otherwise he looked well. "Jane," he said with a smile.

Tears stung her eyes. "I love you," she rasped.

"And I love you," he returned. "I am sorry I doubted you, for you believed in me when no one else did."

She raised her hand and touched the scars on his face. Light shone in his eyes, yet changes had come about in this man. "All is forgiven," she said. "As long as you love and trust me, that is all that matters."

He smiled down at her and then leaned in and kissed her. Her heart and body longed for him, and she ran her hand through his hair, pulling him into her. He was the man she loved, and he had a great affection for her. Nothing would keep them apart ever again. She knew it in her heart.

When the kiss broke, she looked down and laughed when she saw Samuel curled up at the end of the bed.

"He refused to leave your side," Michael explained. "It was the first time the boy has ever refused to heed me, although I must admit I did not expect him to do otherwise in this case."

Jane wiped at her eyes and looked at Michael. "Your brother…"

"Will be brought before the magistrate, as will Catherine. Dalton was escorted out not even an hour ago."

"I am sorry for what he did," she said. "I only wish I would have known sooner."

He shook his head and sighed. "My own guilt blinded me to the truth, so I find it highly doubtful events would have unfolded any differently had you known beforehand." He kissed her hand. "It was my fault and that of no one else. However, those dark days are now gone, and our future is bright ahead of us."

"It is," she said with a smile.

Michael released her hand and stood. "I will take Samuel to his bed now. You must have time to rest. I will return later."

Jane smiled as he leaned in and kissed her brow. When he was gone, she lay back into the pillows and found her mind wandering. For a moment, fear gripped her as images of the fire flickered in her mind, but she stared them down until they melted away into nothing. In that nothingness, a light began to grow, a flame much different from that which had tried to take her life. This light brought her joy and it pulsed with love. And that light was called Michael.

Epilogue

Two weeks passed, and Jane had never been happier. Somehow, Robert and Catherine had managed to escape the magistrates—Michael suspected Robert had paid them off but no proof of this existed—but they had been caught near London as they tried to make their way to Scotland. Their trial would be soon, and Jane suspected that, despite their station, their punishment would be great.

Walking along the cobblestone path in the garden, Jane laughed as Samuel leapt about, calling out for the rabbits. The boy was persistent in his hopes of finding more, and she could not blame him. She had once dreamed of finding a chest full of gold coins, a notion she found silly once she had grown to adulthood. Now, however, she realized she had found her treasure, and he came in the form of a man named Michael. He was her light and her treasure, and she could not imagine a life without him.

That man leaned against the gate that led to the open field behind the garden, smiling at her as he watched her approach. His hair, which he continued to keep long, flowed behind him in the cool breeze, and her heart soared. Yes, she loved this man, but even that word lacked the strength of her feelings for him, for he accentuated that which was best in her and had saved her life in more ways than one. Perhaps no word stronger than love existed; if one did, she did not know it. However, she did not fret over it, for she felt that emotion inside her.

"You wished to see me?" Jane asked.

He took her hands in his and looked down at her. "I did, for there is something I wished to share with you."

Jane's stomach leadened at the seriousness of his tone. Was not all right with the world yet? Did some threat loom over them of which she was unaware?

However, his smile removed all worry, and her stomach righted itself. "I once asked if you would reside in the cottage on my land so I could properly court you," he said. "However, I have come to realize that courting is not something I wish to do."

This time her stomach dropped to her feet. "You do not?" she whispered. How could she have missed a change in his feelings toward her? Had all that had happened to him make him realize that no one could replace Elizabeth, especially a governess?

"No. Only a foolish man would waste his time courting a woman he already loved. A wise man would simply ask the lady if she would marry him."

A wave of affection washed over her, and she had to wipe a tear from her eye. "I see," she replied. "So, are you a foolish or a wise man?"

"Although many may think me foolish," he said, "I do not believe I am. So, Miss Jane Harcourt, I have no doubt that you are the woman I love, and I would be honored if you would become my wife."

Jane smiled up at him. "It would be an honor," she replied.

The next thing she knew, she was in his arms, his lips pressed to hers, and that kiss became stronger and hungrier. Everything in the world seemed to disappear around her, except the man who held her.

Then another pair of arms wrapped around her middle, and she glanced down to see Samuel smiling up at them. She and Michael laughed as they collected the boy in their arms and the trio embraced. Then, with Samuel between them, they gazed out at the sky that displayed a mixture of the pinks, oranges, and reds of one of the most beautiful sunsets Jane had ever experienced in her life.

She must have voiced this sentiment, for Michael turned to her and said, "This might be the most beautiful of sunsets, but you are the most beautiful of women."

Her face had to have reflected the reds in the sky, but her heart soared with the clouds. She was a woman who believed in a man, who in turn, believed in her. A relationship she had been advised would never thrive. Yet, as Anne had counseled, the heart never lies, and Jane's heart told her that she and Michael, along with Samuel, had many long years ahead of them.

About the Author

Much like most Regency authors, Jennifer Monroe fell in love with historical novels of dashing dukes and women wishing to be swept off their feet. She believes that no matter how well a romance story is written, love must be the driving force behind the characters.

Born in France to parents who worked for the United Nations, she found herself traveling the world, until she settled down in New York whilst attending University. As she completed her degree in literature studies, she met and married her loving husband and they soon had two wonderful daughters. She chose to stay home and raise her children, and it was not long before she began to wonder about the novels she loved as a young adult and began to reread some of her favorites. This led her to reading newer authors and eventually to try her hand at writing the stories that bounced around in her head for many years.

Made in the USA
Middletown, DE
01 September 2019